THE GUNDERSON CASE FILES

VOLUME ONE

BLAZE WARD

KNOTTED ROAD PRESS, INC.

The Gunderson Case Files
Volume One
Blaze Ward
Copyright © 2021 Blaze Ward
All rights reserved
Published by Knotted Road Press
www.KnottedRoadPress.com

ISBN: 978-1-64470-226-0

Cover art:

Photo 198260296 / Old Fashioned Detective © Chernetskaya | Dreamstime.com
Illustration 160041801 © Anatolii Riabokon | Dreamstime.com

Cover and interior design copyright © 2021 Knotted Road Press

Reviews
It's true. Reviews help. Even a short one, such as, "Loved it!" So please consider reviewing this book (and all of the ones you've read) on your favorite retailer site.

Never miss a release!
If you'd like to be notified of new releases, sign up for my newsletter.

http://www.blazeward.com/newsletter/

Buy More!
Did you know that you can buy directly from my website?

https://www.blazeward.com/shop/

This book is licensed for your personal enjoyment only. All rights reserved. This is a work of fiction. All characters and events portrayed in this book are fictional, and any resemblance to real people or incidents is purely coincidental. This book, or parts thereof, may not be reproduced in any form without permission.

ALSO BY BLAZE WARD

The Lazarus Alliance

Escape

Return

Rebellion

Revolution

Liberation

Retribution

Alliance

The Jessica Keller Chronicles

Auberon

Queen of the Pirates

Last of the Immortals

Goddess of War

Flight of the Blackbird

The Red Admiral

St. Legier

Winterhome

Petron

CS-405

Queen Anne's Revenge

Packmule

Persephone

Additional Alexandria Station Stories

Siren

Two Bottles of Wine with a War God

The Story Road

The Science Officer Series Season One

The Science Officer

The Mind Field

The Gilded Cage

The Pleasure Dome

The Doomsday Vault

The Last Flagship

The Hammerfield Gambit

The Hammerfield Payoff

The Bryce Connection

The Science Officer Series Season Two

Alien Seas

Shadow of the Dominion

Longshot Hypothesis

Hard Bargain

Outermost

Dominion-427

Phoenix

Princess Rualoh

CONTENTS

INTRODUCTION: GUNDERSON

The inspiration for the character of Gunderson comes from many places, but the voice I hear in my head when he talks is a writer I know. The man would be surprised, but hopefully pleased. (Haven't told him yet.)

The Hard-boiled Private Detective itself is a modern take on the old cowboy or samurai, riding into town and dispensing justice. Dash Hammett did much to bring him into the 20th Century, and set the pace to which the rest of us are merely trying to keep up.

Hollywood then took him and made a few men utterly famous along the way. Humphrey Bogart is so identified with his characters Spade and Marlow that it is occasionally hard to remember he made other movies, but Rick is still my favorite.

When I started down the path of Gunderson, I wanted to do more than just more hard-boiled PI stuff. I write SF generally, and wanted to do something...*strange*. So I moved him to a timeless 1955 instead of setting him in the 1930s or the modern era. It was a different world from both.

Then I looked at the sorts of things being made into

movies in those days, both the Saturday serials and the monster movies. I drew inspiration from the Kolchak television series from the 1970s, envisioning Gunderson as Kolchak's father or uncle, with all the weird shit happening.

Except that in this world, it was all true. Aliens. Monsters. Goddesses. And all the other stuff a smart-mouthed sleuth has to deal with on daily rate and expenses.

Some of these stories are pure SF. Some of them are fantasy of a type I suppose you might call Occult Detective or Period Urban Fantasy (hard to parse those, really). The story **Justice**, which is part of the Gunderson Case Files but not included here, is pure historic. Nothing paranormal or bizarre. Just Gunderson being himself. Seeking Justice. You can find it in the Blaze Ward Presents Anthology #5: "Crime And…"

Also, properly, the genre of mystery requires a crime at the start. That crime must be resolved by the end. Not necessarily solved, mind you. Merely *Resolved*.

That's what Gunderson does. He's just a guy who's really good solving puzzles and finding answers. At the same time, I wanted to give him flaws that were a-typical for the genre those more realistic for his era. Too many of the PIs in print are broken-down bums who put away too much whiskey in order to sleep at the things they've seen.

Gunderson is not. He was broken by World War Two. Most of the men who served and came home were able to compartmentalize themselves, but not all. My own grandfather had stories that he didn't tell anyone until I asked him in the late 70s as part of a school project. Hard stories, because he was part of a unit that liberated one of the concentration camps in southern Germany.

Gunderson came back and couldn't be a cop anymore. Didn't want Seattle. Ended up as a PI in L.A., because that's what someone of his size and skills was good at.

He can't save the world, but that won't stop him from trying. These are six of the first seven stories, and I have notes for many more.

Come, see what the world is like for an ex-cop doing the hardest job in the world.

Surviving…

WANDERING MONSTERS

THE GUNDERSON CASE FILES (001)
WANDERING MONSTERS

EVERYONE CALLED him Gunderson these days.

Sure, his mom still called him Eugene, but few other people did. A couple of childhood friends had once called him Gene, but he hadn't seen any of them since before the War, and he'd never been back to Seattle since Hitler and Tojo got run out of town.

A daring few people had even been so bold as to take his initials and call him *Gigi*, like some French tart. He'd met a few after helping kick Hitler's ass. Gunderson even let a couple of pretty women call him that today.

The last marine that had made that mistake still walked with a limp.

He studied the noon-day sun running across the brown whateverness of the Port of Los Angeles just beyond the cyclone fence, as he closed the door of his old, battered '49 Mallory coupe and decided that it wasn't going to get any better today. Or worse.

Spring sun, with occasional trouble.

But Gunderson was in the trouble business. Freelance these days though. He'd been a cop before Pearl Harbor.

Enlisted like all the other patriotic fools in December '41. Ended up as an MP rather than driving tanks like he'd wanted. Military life wasn't that much different than civilian, just with fewer *femme fatales* around.

Civilian world had more of them, but he was still dealing with hard-headed punks most of the time these days.

Nine years home and the world had finally generally settled down. He even liked Ike, but all the pretty, rich people in this town occasionally still needed tall, blond, rough-looking Swedes like him to take care of trouble.

Some men had come home from the war and started families. Boom of babies gonna take over the world one of these days. Others had come home broken. Some bad. Some worse.

Gunderson had managed to be not-too-broken, but not so perfect either. Didn't want a badge again after all that. Still carried a gun.

Odds of him needing it in here today were probably even, but he wasn't going to be dealing with blackmailers or hopheads. Just a favor for an old friend. One who was even allowed to call him *Gigi*.

He stuffed the hat down on his head, wondering if he should have gotten his hair cut this morning so it fit better. Lots of things had gone a little slack lately, but he had a hard time caring. Get up, make coffee, maybe have a cigarette or three, go do things.

Gunderson crossed the parking lot to the joint that was today's issue. The whole neighborhood was a little dead, but that was the US Army deploying around the Port area to deal with some new monster issue. He hadn't even bothered turning on the radio on the way over here, because all those announcers were going to do was self-importantly or breathlessly tell people to either stay in their homes or flee out the freeway and try to make it someplace like Berdoo or

Needles, depending on what the hell was wanting to come ashore. And where.

Another kaiju or something. Papers had been vague yesterday. Lurid, like all good yellow journalism, but that was just to sell papers. Navy wasn't talking and the Marines were supposedly coming up from Pendleton to help the Army handle things.

He'd been able to slip a fin to the Sergeant at the blockade to be let through. Helped that he'd served with the guy in Africa and France, once upon a yesterday.

So here he was. Micky's place. *The Rum Runner*, although nobody needed to run booze up from Ensenada anymore. Hopheads smuggled smack these days, but that wasn't his thing and nobody hired him to kidnap their kids or husbands to get them into detox.

He'd done that a few times. Man got positively rude as those jitters came in. The screaming as they laid there, strapped down and biting at the leather bit in their mouth had put Gunderson off that kind of work. Hope to God he was never that broke again.

Only a few other cars in the big lot, but Mickey's really didn't wind itself up until dinner time, even on a normal day. Probably a prep crew that had been doing food work for dinner trapped inside the Army blockade and unable to get out. Or afraid to run.

Nobody knew where the damned thing was headed. Or the Navy did and wasn't telling. They could be like that. Another reason he'd gone into the Army instead.

Gunderson stepped up onto the long, concrete porch now and studied the door. Done once upon a time in early South Seas chic with faux palm leaves made out of steel and etchings of hula girls. Probably about the time he was born. Not long before the old restaurant had been turned into a kind of speak-easy dinner club. The Twenties had been weird and exotic, even in Los Angeles, but he'd been a kid then. He hadn't started being a Seattle cop until Prohibition was over, and then only a detective for two years before the War changed everything. For a lot of folks.

He put a big mitt on the handle and pulled the heavy wood panel open. Wasn't locked, but that was probably an oversight on their part. He didn't mind. Made his life easier.

Dark inside. Rank with sour cigarette smoke, like they should have opened all the doors and let the place air out. Air conditioning was on, but not drawing enough of the outside air in. Port of Los Angeles didn't stink that bad. Old asphalt and ripe fish.

Throw in a little coconut-flavored sunscreen and you had the California Dream.

Gunderson stepped into the place and let the door swing shut behind him, looking around as he could see better.

"Bar's closed," an angry voice yelled as his eyes slowly adjusted inside.

Station in front of him for a hostess, at least on swanky nights. Currently abandoned. Two arms of booths going away at ninety degrees. A few steps down to a hardwood floor in the middle with tables and a spot on the left for a dance floor, just in front of a stage too small for a real bandstand.

Gunderson wondered if they brought in Jitterbug acts or maybe that Rock and Roll the kids were listening too these days. Something to try to draw in the crowds.

Big bar across the back, fronted with permanent stools on swiveling posts with low backs. All of them were empty. Bartender was behind it, a short, pudgy guy wiping it down with a rag and wearing a loud, floral print shirt that made Gunderson's off-the-rack brown jacket look formal and expensive. Hard to tell from here what kind of swarthy the guy was as Gunderson set off that way. Maybe Italian. Lot of those in Southern California these days. Possibly a Mexican who's family had woke up one day a century ago and discovered that they were Americans now. Plenty of families like that in Los Angeles, too, tracing things back to when the Spanish first arrived and the United States was still just a twinkle in ol' Ben Franklin's eye.

"Said we're closed, dumb ass," the bartender sneered as Gunderson crossed the dance floor.

Skin and hair said Mexican. Accent was pure Los Angeles.

Gunderson saw two faces in a kitchen behind the bar, through a window off to the left. They were all looking in his direction, but had that bright, shiny, useless look of prep cooks. Kids nobody trusted with a stove yet.

He'd been there, too.

Man did a lot of things after he was finished with the Army if he didn't want to go back to a badge. Cooking hadn't worked out either.

"Looking for someone," Gunderson rumbled back at the bartender.

He had about eight inches on the man and probably fifty pounds, so the cooks would need to come up from the back if they really wanted to try throwing him out. Welcome to try.

But Gunderson figured he should always try the easy way at least once. Mama always said you caught more flies with honey than you did vinegar, so he slipped onto a stool and pushed a dollar bill across the bar.

Bartender looked at it like Gunderson had just taken a ----- on the counter, then looked up at him.

"You're going to be a pain in my ass, aren't you?" the man asked.

Both hands were in sight, so Gunderson wasn't worried about him coming up with a gun or a baseball bat. The joint didn't have that kind of a rep anymore. Like the rest of Los Angeles, they'd gone straight when Prohibition ended.

Straighter, anyway. It was still Mickey's joint and that spooked some people.

"I'm here to see Mickey," Gunderson smiled. "I don't have an appointment, but we aren't any of us going anywhere for a while, are we?"

"You're nuts, *pendejo*, you know that?"

Gunderson shrugged. Not the first time he'd been called either, even this week.

"There's a monster supposed to come ashore this afternoon," the bartender snapped. "You know, giant radioactive swimming lizard thing, like they got in the movies? Don't you listen to the radio?"

"Gives me indigestion," Gunderson cracked wise right back at the guy. "They keep interrupting the Cleveland Orchestra playing Mozart to tell me that nobody knows what the thing is, or where it's at, or what part of L.A. is supposed to be flattened this time."

He watched the bartender's eyes narrow. Mostly a good sulk and scowl, rather than a tell that things were about to get messy in here. Guy looked too young to have seen the war from the inside. Probably thought bar fights were clean, pretty things, like they did in Hollywood just up the highway, rather than bloody scrums filled with drunks so numb that they might bleed out on the floor and never notice it.

Gunderson smiled at the kid.

Honey. Vinegar.

"Mickey's not here."

"His car's out in the parking lot," Gunderson replied brightly. "And the Army is already locking things down, so none of us are going anywhere until either that beast flattens the joint or they bring in some big-brain inventor with a super weapon to kill it. You could save me a lot of time and yourself a bunch of heartburn. Just wander back to Mickey's office and tell him he has a caller. Assuming he's not peeking at me through a mirror or something already."

Gunderson would have felt better if there was a big mirror on the back bar, so nobody could sneak up on him except vampires, but it had been broken a couple of times in the old days and was too expensive for the insurance company to want to replace again. Instead, they'd just built up shelves for liquor bottles back there now.

He pulled a fin and slid it onto the bar, not far from the bill already there.

"You could fill me a shot of Kentucky Rye before you go, if you wanted to be hospitable," he said breezily.

Honey. Vinegar.

The bartender just stood there for a long second, more grumpy than angry.

Finally, he swept both bills off the back of the counter and grabbed a highball glass that would look clean with the lights down dim. Bottle came up from the shelf under the bar, but Gunderson didn't figure he was going to get the top-shelf stuff anyway. The pour was respectable enough.

And this looked like a peace offering between strangers.

Gunderson toasted the man as the fellow started down the bar towards a door opposite the kitchen. Back where the bathrooms and office were. Mickey's office, although Gunderson had never been in there.

Joyce had told him the layout of the whole place when she asked for a favor for her friend Caroline. The kind of favor that needed a big, dumb Swede who occasionally carried a gun.

She was one of the few who got to call him *Gigi*.

Outside, an Army truck was finally making the rounds. Or again. The kind with a big public address speaker on the roof so fancy Majors could get up there and fire up the troops who'd maybe gotten a little burned out on all the blood they spilled from places as far back as Kasserine.

"Attention, citizens of Los Angeles."

Or at least it sounded like that. Place had pretty good sound-proofing going on, so Gunderson was listening to the rhythm as much as the words themselves.

"By order of the Mayor and the Governor, you are ordered to immediately evacuate the area, heading north or east," the man with the loud voice continued. "This area is under martial law."

Gunderson chuckled to himself. Considering how corrupt most of the cops in this county were, martial law was probably three steps up. Too bad they wouldn't take advantage of that power to clean a few places up and maybe hang a couple of people that really needed it. Didn't need to send many men to the gas chamber to do the trick, as long as the rest learned.

Or joined them.

But Gunderson wasn't trying to save the world anymore. His own soul was too much of a burden, so he was reduced to favors for Joyce and her friend. At least the money was good.

Gunderson took a sip of the rye as the man outside repeated himself, slowly rolling down the street, and decided that maybe the fin had been worth it. Better than you got in most of the joints in Tijuana unless they charged you American prices for it.

The bartender emerged from that back hallway with a scowl on his face that promised trouble later, but gestured with one hand for Gunderson to head back that way.

Gunderson took his glass. He'd been overcharged for the booze, so he might as well drink it all.

A glance and the two cooks were back to chopping.

Presumably, if the neighborhood survived a giant, radioactive swimming lizard monster, people would want to drink and dance and maybe forget their lives for a while.

Gunderson wondered if the damned thing just wanted to lay its eggs in peace but kept getting hassled by the silly humans.

Also, not his fight, so he walked down the front of the bar and turned the corner to follow the bartender into the narrow, dark hallway.

There was a door open back there, spilling light into the hallway like a dying man stains the linoleum as he bleeds out. Gunderson looked down on the top of the bartender's head but the fellow stopped at the doorway, slid to one side, and gestured Gunderson in.

He smiled at the man and made sure neither hand had a sap in it. Maybe stepped a little quicker around the fellow and into the office.

"Close the door," Mickey said as Gunderson got clear of it.

The bartender reached in and pulled it shut.

"Sit down," came the order.

Gunderson picked the chair that looked to have fewer stains on the leather.

Mickey Lombardi sat on the other side of a huge desk. Oak. The kind corporate tycoons owned, in order to tell you how important they were. Or how well-endowed. Gunderson had never quite figured that one out.

Big man, but only in the sense that he was wide, with florid skin that might look like the bartender's cousin until you got close and realized his parents had been Wops. Maybe grandparents.

Not connected with the old country crime syndicates, but Los Angeles had its own versions and connections, for men with the gumption.

Dark hair a little long and slicked back, which was unfortunate because it showed off the gray roots that hadn't been dyed in a week or so. Button nose going bulbous with drink and age. Skin showing the ravages of something more than cheap bourbon, but that was none of Gunderson's problem. If the man was a hophead, Joyce hadn't mentioned it. Or didn't know.

Nice suit. Tailored in gunmetal gray silk, back about fifteen pounds ago. Red silk tie was cutting into his flabby neck like the hangman's noose a fellow like Mickey probably deserved. Shoes under the desk likely cost as much as Gunderson's second-hand jalopy out front had run him.

The room was like that. Brag wall on the left, showing Mickey entertaining mayors, councilmen, and two governors, along with a nice slice of Hollywood folk down from the hills to slum with the port denizens.

Gunderson settled into the chair, hoping that someone had wiped the leather down from the last wanna-be starlet that had come in desperate for a job and gotten talked into things that would make her mother swoon. Maybe that was why the man needed a big desk. Lots of space for those sorts of gymnastics with the door closed. No windows in here for folks to spy anything untoward.

And Mickey Lombardi was all about the *untoward*.

Gunderson smiled and rested his last finger of rye on the near edge of the desk.

Mickey had a similar glass on his side, next to his left hand and filled with a prettier cut of something.

The right hand was resting on an old Colt Officer's model. Gunderson would have figured the man for a Luger or something, but Mickey Lombardi had never seen his patriotic duty emerge, unless crooked game rooms and whiskey cut with water counted.

Man wasn't holding the gun, but could have it in his

hands fast enough. Gunderson didn't figure he could actually lift the desk and throw it at the man all that fast.

Wasn't the same as taking his time later, if he needed to. But Gunderson had showered, shaved, and put on the nice cologne this morning. The bottle from another one of those girls who got to call him *Gigi* when she was in town.

Mickey smelled a little like day old sweat and desperation.

"Was kind of surprised to find you and the crew working this morning," Gunderson began out of the blue. "What with the Army chasing everyone off. Place is likely to be a battleground this afternoon. Lots of buildings might get smooshed."

Mickey had a tell.

A little twitch at the outer edge of his left eyeball. Not a wink, because he wasn't smiling, but the whole left side of his face spasmed for a moment.

"What do you want, flatfoot?" Mickey said in a voice that probably would have been impressive it if hadn't been a high tenor better suited to a boys choir.

"No badge these days," Gunderson corrected him. "Private dick. Jobs for folks with money and needs. Not interested in upholding the law."

"Then what the hell do you want?" Mickey growled in that squeaky voice.

"Oh, I'd like to say I'm here to see a man about a horse." Gunderson said with a hard grin. "But I'm on a job. Looking for a man."

"Blackmailer or straying husband?"

The left hand picked up that glass so Mickey could take a minuscule sip. The right hand never moved.

"Little of both," Gunderson replied with a knowing nod. "Hard man to track down when he wants to hide from folks. But I figured I could start here and maybe ask around a little.

After all, we're sitting in the shadow of the latest doom to befall the golden city. The City Fathers just finished rebuilding the Hollywood sign after the last time. Nobody's going to be moving around much, especially not with the Army folks outside keen to arrest everyone to get them out of the way."

More twitch. Most of what Gunderson was talking was pure hokum right now, but he'd learned a long time ago the value of good conversation to smooth things out. Cut down on the misunderstandings, especially when a man had a big .45 close at hand and maybe nerves that were starting to wear thin in places.

Outside, a dull thump turned into a whole series of them. Muffled by more than distance.

Gunderson wondered if the Navy had flown a bunch of planes over and dropped depth charges on something. Old dive bombers weren't all that useful these days, but a lizard swimming along wouldn't be shooting back. Probably.

Mickey flinched to the rhythm of the crumps. To Gunderson, it almost sounded like a wall of 75s lighting up a German battalion with a time-on-target barrage, every gun firing in a sequence calculated by distance, so that all the shells landed at the same time. Pure murder if you caught infantry in the open that way.

"Kinda hoping that the battle goes south into the orange groves," Gunderson said as Mickey stared at him with a little bit of hatred.

But Gunderson had invaded his home turf this morning. Maybe bringing bad luck and a giant radioactive swimming lizard with him.

Weirder things had happened.

"Be a shame if the beast turned north and stomped on all these buildings and things," Gunderson continued in a voice better suited to wild animals than Wop gangsters. If there was a difference. "Hopefully the insurance companies won't have to pay out a lot for this mess."

Eye-twitch again.

Gunderson wondered if Mickey had let his building insurance lapse. There'd been rumors of financial difficulties around here. Maybe the place would be a smoking ruin by evening? Certainly can't torch the place for the insurance money if there wasn't any.

Heart-breaking. Really

Still not Gunderson's problem.

"So who are you looking for, punk?" Mickey cut to the chase finally.

"You, Mickey," Gunderson said brightly, hands on the arms of his chair, out in the open.

The gat still came up in the flicker of an eye. Barrel on a .45 looked huge when you staring up it, wondering if the idiot holding it had remembered to chamber a round.

Folks used to carrying old revolvers frequently left an empty spot under the hammer when they carried it, in case they dropped it and the damned thing went off. Limited you to only five shots, so you had to be prepared to reload faster.

Officer's Model could be carried with an extra round in the barrel, hammer back, and the safety holding everything safe enough. Plus, it was a lot of gun if you had to whip someone across the face with it.

"What's your game, punk?" Mickey hissed snappily. Then he raised his voice. "Get in here!"

Gunderson heard the door behind him open and glanced back enough to know that it was the bartender, holding a little snub .38 like Gunderson used to carry, when it went with his badge.

Compact, but had a tendency to just knock a man down for a little bit.

Gunderson liked to tell people that he fell in love with a

man right after he shot him, so it pained him to have to shoot someone he loved.

Which was why he carried a big .44 under his arm.

Still, he didn't move right now. Both of the locals were a little too keen for violence for a club owner and a bartender.

But this was *The Rum Runner*. Not exactly on the up and up, as it were. Even for Los Angeles.

"Came to see you, Mickey," Gunderson said without moving anything but his lips. "Got a message for you. Nothing more. Nobody else wanted to deliver it, on account of your rep in this town."

"Brace him," Mickey ordered the bartender.

"Smith & Wesson Model 29 under my left arm in a shoulder rig," Gunderson said pleasantly. "Left the rest at home this morning."

Which was only slightly a lie. There were two in the Mallory, but they were out in the parking lot, about as close as Mars right now.

Bartender came around his left and held that .38 a little too close and sloppy for a pro, but Gunderson wasn't here as an assassin.

Well, not a physical one, anyone. Social, maybe. Difference of degree.

Still, he let the Mexican take the cannon, for now. He'd get it back before he left.

One way or the other.

"Stand up," the bartender ordered, so Gunderson did, looming over both men with a breezy smile on his face. "Don't move."

Sloppy job of looking for a second gun, but Gunderson wasn't surprised. Fool never even looked around his ankles, where he occasionally shipped a .25 automatic.

"He's clean," the man said.

Bartender stepped back and placed the .44 on the desk, closer to Mickey's side, but far enough away for now.

"Okay, wise guy, what's this all about?" Mickey demanded in a shrill voice just this side of a teapot boiling.

"I'd like to pull some papers from the right inside pocket," Gunderson said. "Without getting shot in the process."

That was an unfortunate turn of phrase right now. Somewhere in the distance, Gunderson heard what sounded like a quad .50 anti-aircraft halftrack or two open up. Maybe just every M2 machine gun the Army had in the armory this week.

Lots of copper-jacketed lead suddenly going downrange. He hoped that the lizard wasn't between him and the shooters.

Incoming fire could be a bitch.

Mickey flinched pretty hard and glanced at the ceiling as the hard rumble of machine gun fire intruded. The bartender turned to look into the invisible distance in awe, but he didn't look like a soldier. A little too 4H about him.

Gunderson kept that in mind.

Both still had guns pointed at him and Gunderson didn't really have a reason to get shot today. At least not by these two punks. Ex-wives and old partners he'd found in bed together were a different story.

"Go on," Mickey sneered now, gesturing with the Colt like it was a magic wand or something.

Lot of fools made that mistake. Thought that pointing a gun at someone was the way to get them to do things.

Asking was always a smarter option.

In the end, he was here because nobody else would deal with Mickey Lombardi and his trouble. Even in the middle of a kaiju battling the US Army just down the street.

Gunderson reached delicately inside his jacket with his left hand and pulled out a trifold of papers with two fingers.

In the background, heavier artillery started to crump, but he wasn't getting the whistle of shells falling on his position, so maybe it was just tanks firing their main guns at the creature while it wanted to clear a spot to bury some eggs.

Then there was the sound of Stukas coming over the top. Or maybe Navy Dauntless dive bombers. That was a particular sound as that sucker started his run.

"What's that?" Mickey yelled over the increasing din of warfare.

Gunderson wondered if the lizard would squish his Mallory. No great loss. And it was insured for this sort of thing. Maybe he'd move up to a Brubaker sedan or something next time.

Rather than answer, Gunderson looked up at the ceiling, as if hearing the noise of the first time.

There, the relative silence of a plane suddenly leveling off and then climbing back out.

Gunderson counted in his head.

"Got some paperwork for you, Mickey," he said loudly. Not loud enough for the man to do more than read lips, but that was the idea. Get him focused by talking too quiet and waving some papers in the air.

The bombs went off. Sounded close enough that the bodega on the corner might be flattened right now, throwing shattered fruit and cans of beer everywhere.

The sound was literally Earth-shattering. Gunderson had been through enough earthquakes around L.A. to feel that same rolling as everything moved. The sound of the bombs striking the ground was a solid wave tsunami coming up the beach and slamming into your chest.

Good thing Gunderson had known it was coming.

He dropped the papers on the desk as the other two men cringed away from the sound.

A stiff-arm into the bartender's face bounced the man off the wall as Gunderson knocked the pistol out of his hand.

Mickey had frozen in terror, and was only now starting to turn to follow Gunderson's movement as the tall Swede came around the desk. One big, right paw clenched up and hammered the side of Mickey's head like the man with the hammer greeting the cattle at the slaughterhouse.

The sound would have been just as sickening, but the fourth and fifth bombs going off covered everything right now.

Mickey's head cracking on the surface of his desk was a visual cue, like a movie where the speakers have suddenly died and just hissed static at the auditorium.

Gunderson took the Officer's Model out of Mickey's unresisting hand and stuffed his big, black .44 revolver back into his jacket. He stepped back around the desk about the time the bartender stopped sliding down the wall. He kicked the .38 into a far corner like a puck, back when he went to see the Seattle Metropolitans play as a kid.

Then Gunderson chased that puck down and stuffed it into a pocket of his jacket, turning back to the rest of the room about the time the sound fell to nothing.

The bartender started to scramble to his feet, but stopped when Gunderson stuck the pistol in his face.

Gunderson smiled.

"Pull a chair over and have a seat so I don't feel like I have to shoot you right now," he offered the man grimly.

Bartender complied, probably aware of whose story the cops in this town would believe, if a white man shot a Wop and a Mexican and called it self-defense. Most of the force was Irish these days.

Gunderson picked up what was left of his rye with his

offhand and drank it down as Mickey started to stir. There was a small puddle of blood and slobber on the desk from where he'd probably broken his nose. Looked broken when he finally leaned back enough to look up at the death looming over him right now.

"See, Mickey, you had to be an asshole," Gunderson said simply. "I hadn't given you any cause, but you don't need any, do you?"

The eyes were only a little glassy, but the bartender could fill the man in on the details later.

Gunderson set the empty glass down softly and nodded to the bartender. Peace offering.

Honey. Vinegar.

"So Mickey Lombardi, I hereby declare that I have served you these papers," Gunderson picked up the trifold bundle and slid it across to the stupid gangster in the expensive suit. "Caroline demands a divorce from you, and if you do not contest it in court, she won't turn state's evidence in the process. Personally, I think you're getting off easy, because that woman could probably put you away forever and get everything you own in the deal if she wanted to go up in front of a grand jury and testify in court. You coherent enough to follow what I'm saying?"

"Yeah," Mickey snarled, but there wasn't any heat behind it. And he didn't move to stop the blood flowing down from that cracked nose and ruining that suit that he already should have gotten rid of.

"Good," Gunderson continued. "Any questions?"

"Lemme tell you, punk..."

"Mickey, if I ever see you or him again, I'm going to open fire and assume it was self-defense when I kill you," Gunderson interrupted. "If you were a smart man, you'd sell this place and move to Texas or someplace where I can guarantee I'd never come visit. Caroline doesn't want anything right now but her freedom, so you'll leave her alone as well, or you'll answer to me. And all my friends in this town. Are we clear?"

Mickey just scowled at him, but nodded after a long pause. No man likes looking up the barrel of his own gun in the hands of an angry Swede.

Gunderson turned to the bartender to include the man in the threat, but he didn't figure he'd need to hunt the man. Punk was just an employee.

Outside, the air had turned to silence, so maybe the Air Force or Navy had managed to kill the beast before it got too far inland. Why things wanted to destroy Los Angeles was lost on Gunderson, but he supposed that maybe the angels had taken a particular dislike to the town.

"I'm leaving," Gunderson announced to the two of them. "Don't follow so I don't have to kill either of you. Maybe you should leave town soon, though."

Gunderson didn't wait for any answer from the men. The bomb blasts had knocked the door open, but there weren't any windows in here to spray shattered glass.

He stepped into the hallway and pulled the door shut. There was an icemaker at the end of the bar. Gunderson popped the magazine out of the handle and pocketed it, then worked the slide and caught the bullet flying. He tossed the hunk of iron into the ice and closed the panel up again, wondering if they'd find it before the thing rusted solid and ruined however many drinks got made before they did.

He kept the .38. He could always sell it. Or turn it over the cops and tell them where he'd found it. Might tie it to a few crimes after they looked at the ballistics.

Windows on the front were all gone from the overpressure, but he'd been expecting that. He ignored the window to the kitchen and crossed the dance floor, out that heavy door and into the afternoon sun.

The angels must like him, he thought, as Mickey's Phaeton had been crushed under a block of concrete about the size of a coffin, while the old Mallory didn't even look to be more dusty than an hour ago.

Dead silence outside, but he heard a few birds starting to chirp again as he climbed in and started the beast.

Hopefully, this emergency was over, and Los Angeles could get back to normal.

Not that he believed it for a moment.

But he'd be here to pick up the pieces. That was what he did.

THE MAN WHO KNOWS

THE GUNDERSON CASE FILES (002)
THE MAN WHO KNOWS

GUNDERSON WAS down the street at his favorite bar. He kept an office. Law said he had to. Place to display his Private Investigator license and keep a couple of old file cabinets with the bits and pieces of cases that he'd bothered writing down and keeping.

A lot of what he did was better off not being recorded, as long as he kept scrupulous financial records and payed everybody the right taxes and occasional bribes.

Most of his business came in from referrals rather than walk-ins. Friends of friends sort of thing. In Gunderson's experience, whenever a beautiful dame walked in out of the blue it almost always turned into a bad movie script or a lurid whodunit novel, and he really didn't have the patience with people to put up with that malarkey these days.

He rarely kept actual office hours for the same reason, instead hiring Annabelle, a retired friend of a friend who had been a welder grandma during the war, to mostly babysit said office and knit or read weird books. Today, it had been a text book on architecture of mid-1600s London. Last week it had been how to build your own liquid-fueled rocket. She was like that.

Still, he trusted her judgment.

So when Annabelle had called the bar where he'd been playing pool and told him to haul his ass back to the office, he'd handed the other guy a bill and walked.

The woman sitting in his office right now looked like trouble when he got past Annabelle and her bulwark of a yarn-covered desk and stack of books. Gunderson got an eyefull of the stranger, wondering if he'd wandered into a b-movie accidentally or something.

She was that beautiful.

Tall when she rose to greet him. Gunderson was six-foot-three, plus shoes on their second sole and third heel. The bombshell was in six inch heels and looked him in the eye.

Long, auburn hair under a net that was attached to a hat a little too big to be a fascinator, but probably was anyway. Black and silk and pretty, anyway.

She wore a steel-gray skirt with a matching jacket cut more like a man's, with a starched white shirt. Cute little ribbon in place of a tie. Stockings.

Money. And trouble.

At least she shook his hand firmly as he got her into his office.

Gunderson took his seat on the other side of the desk.

"Good afternoon," he said. "Name's Gunderson."

"Matilda Dubois," she replied, saying it the French way but without any accent.

Rock on her left hand said *Mrs.* He wasn't going to make any other assumptions right now.

"And what can I do for you, Mrs. Dubois?" Gunderson asked.

"It's my husband," she said before pausing.

Gunderson particularly didn't like cases where the wife

suspected a husband of having an affair. Hard enough to prove that the dog never barked, unless you caught him in the act.

Gunderson had never been much of a voyeur.

But he smiled at her. Money was money, and she had a lot of it, just from the way she was dressed. And smelled.

"Oh?" he prompted after she took a moment, maybe finding the words. "Suspect he's having an affair?"

"If only it could be something so simple," she replied.

And he had to agree. Man cheating on a woman this beautiful was a fool. Or maybe she was just a complete ----- and the husband had found someone more hospitable.

Gunderson had known a few couples like that. Political marriage kind of thing, but providing one with financial stability and the other companionship instead of establishing peace between kingdoms.

"So what is the problem?" Gunderson asked.

"I think he's a spy," Mrs. Dubois said. "Maybe working for the Communists or someone. No, if he was just seeing another woman I could find a way to tolerate that."

Gunderson took a deep breath and considered it. Certainly more fun than a case of infidelity. And the way she was dressed said that she had money to handle his daily rate and expenses, probably out of pocket change.

"Okay," he decided. "Tell me about it."

WHICH WAS how Gunderson ended up sitting in a parking lot across the street from an old Masonic Lodge on a Wednesday night with a camera. Gunderson knew cameras well enough to load film and shoot pretty good pictures when he needed to.

His buddy Clayton had told Gunderson more than once

that he had the eye to become a professional if he wanted, but to Gunderson that sounded too much like work. He liked being his own boss. However, Clayton still owed him a few for saving his ass from some things better left unsaid in polite company, and had gifted him with a camera bag full of parts left over whenever the man upgraded.

Gunderson refused to learn the lingo of photo nerds, flat out. Couldn't tell you why, but it all just rubbed him the wrong way.

Instead, he had the settings memorized as Night, Haze, and Sunlight. Lenses for close, medium, far. Nighttime-window from across the street and from pressed up against the glass. He'd even labeled them that way in the bag, just so he could tell someone else, if he ever had someone sitting next to him in his old '49 Mallory coupe while he was on a stakeout.

Not tonight, but Gunderson was a man who believed in planning ahead.

Émile Dubois drove a big four-door in blue. Almost brand new, like a lot of the cars parked over there, but he hadn't arrived yet. Wasn't supposed to, but Gunderson knew that this was the case to prove the dog didn't bark. Painful, but he was getting paid well for his time and expenses, and this was just going to be a few hours tonight.

He'd considered the Masonic Order a few times, but they were always a little too John Birch for him. He didn't believe for a second all the bizarre conspiracy theories rumored, if only because a conspiracy that big wasn't a conspiracy anymore. It had turned into a government. And he'd forgotten the count of how many Masons had signed the Declaration of Independence, but it was a bunch of them.

So he kept watch for a blue four-door he wasn't expecting, going so far as to track any car that drove down this block but didn't turn in. At the appointed time, the doors were all closed up and the building went quiet. A few hours later, all the men in nicer suits than his filed out, chatting with one another before getting into their cars and heading home to loving families.

At least that was how the story went. He'd shot a couple of pictures, just to justify his time in case Mrs. Dubois asked, but he got the impression she wouldn't.

Didn't want to go to the police with her suspicions, on account that Émile had to have friends in City Hall and she really didn't know who they might be.

French Industrialist who had escaped before the Nazis arrived and eventually settled in the States. Married a beautiful woman two decades younger than him and kept her in style. Matilda had been an aspiring actress who managed to get recruited by Émile instead of a producer.

Gunderson had been in this town long enough to know how lucky the woman was on that score. Most of those starlets got to discover just how seedy Hollywood really was before they managed to escape.

Those of them that did.

Matilda Dubois might need a different kind of escape.

Gunderson packed everything up after the parking lot emptied and headed home. He had other cases to work before he circled back to this one.

GUNDERSON WALKED into his office pretty early this morning, but Annabelle was already there. She always got up early enough to get the first donuts, hot out of the oil, and then came into the office as the sun was coming up. Today she was reading Plato, but he couldn't tell what language it had been written in. Wasn't English.

He didn't ask. She didn't volunteer.

Widow the last four years or so, she didn't mind his hours and didn't really need the job for more than a reason to get out of the house. Kinda like him, except that nobody had left him a pension.

"Second Wednesday of the month," she reminded him as he entered. "Mr. Dubois's lodge meeting is tonight."

"Thank you," he said as he carried his coffee and newspaper into his inner sanctum.

Inside, he pulled out a mapbook and studied the region. The Dubois household was out in Pasadena, in an upper class neighborhood where bankers and industrialists might live, instead of actors or movie moguls who were generally further west. Much more buttoned down kind of place, where his Mallory would stand out if he tried to just park and watch the house.

Even a big Swede like him would have a police car roll up after a few minutes with a cop who politely rapped on his window and demanded to know what the hell he was up to.

But he'd scouted it a few times in the last month. Just driven through without slowing down enough to give the neighbors any sort of heartburn. There was an all-night joint more or less on the main drag out of the neighborhood. Soda fountain and hot plate in addition to an apothecary, so folks occasionally sat and had dinner when they didn't want to be home. Or maybe worked for one of the rich families up the hill and were on their way to their own home.

There were no children in the Dubois household, so only one live-in maid. According to Mrs. Dubois, her husband was apparently sterile, so they could have marital relations, but never children.

She hadn't seemed particularly put out by that, but Gunderson wasn't all that surprised. The woman had come across a little cold and calculating, but her money spent just as well as anyone else's, and she had a big retainer paid up front that covered the strange surveillance he would have to pull on this case.

From what Gunderson had gathered, the couple had spent more time in the sack early on, but it had waned over the last few years. He wondered if one of them had gotten tired of it and just not told the other. She had looked like a woman who might have done something about it, but they didn't have a pool to have a pool boy.

Again, not his problem. If the man was a spy instead of just off philandering, she'd need evidence. And connections about who to talk to, although she hadn't hired him to handle that.

Gunderson amended that to *yet* and went back to his paper.

LATE AFTERNOON, Gunderson found himself at that store at the bottom of the hill from the Dubois neighborhood. He'd gone ahead and ordered an open-faced roast beast sandwich from the available options. He showed the man behind the counter his PI license and slipped him a fin, explaining that he was on surveillance tonight.

The man had nodded, neither here nor there, and gone over to cook. Then ignored him after that.

Gunderson stepped into the closest telephone booth, memorizing the number as he dialed the Dubois household.

"Mrs. Dubois, please," he said to the woman who answered. "This is Mr. Gunderson, from the tailor. She asked us to call when a certain lot of fabric arrived."

It had been an easy enough code to set up. The maid wouldn't know any better and it let him call without trying to impersonate anybody. All her suits were bespoke anyway.

"Hello?" she asked as she came on the line.

Gunderson didn't hear anyone clicking the line as they picked up an extension, but he knew how easy that sort of thing was to hide.

"Mrs. Dubois, this is Mr. Gunderson at your tailor's. He asked me to call and let you know that the fabric you had asked about was in. Is this a good time?"

"It is not, actually," she replied. "Can I call you back?"

"Certainly," he said, giving her the number where he was at.

"Thank you," and she hung up.

Gunderson waited in the booth, just in case. After a few moments, the man behind the counter waved and slipped a plate over, refilling his coffee as well, so Gunderson ate. As long as that phone didn't ring, he was in good shape.

He killed an hour, reading a couple of newspapers and smoking a few cigarettes. A couple of folks came and went, one colored woman even stopping for a hot sandwich. Gunderson had seen her approaching and moved himself clear down to the far end of the counter with a nod of apology that seemed to surprise her, but not him.

California had a reputation for progressivism that rivaled places like Kansas. There were still pockets out in the Inland Empire or up north where they weren't just still fighting the Civil War, but still losing. In a different neighborhood, he could see her not even being allowed to eat with a white person.

She ate warily anyway, and Gunderson did his best to ignore her like just another stranger met on a train platform.

The phone rang and he slipped off his stool, pulling the accordion door closed as he stepped in.

"White's Tailoring, Mr. Gunderson speaking," he said, still playing a role.

"This is Matilda Dubois," she said simply. "He left about five minutes ago."

"Very good," he said.

She hung up immediately and he did the same. Outside, he left another buck on the counter, nodded to the wary woman eating her mashed potatoes, and went out into the parking lot.

Most of the traffic was headed uphill this time of night. Men going home from work to a family dinner. The black woman inside had surprised him, because as a rule the help would not depart until after dinner, perhaps staying extremely late into the evening and then not getting home before midnight.

He got into his heap and watched as the blue four-door came rolling down the hill at a sedate pace commensurate with a wealthy investor and industrialist going to a meeting with his accountant. Gunderson started his engine and pulled out, timing it so that Émile had a reasonable lead on an empty-enough road.

Down they went. Gunderson had a moment of panic when Émile got onto old Route 66 and headed east, so he closed up and tried to only keep a few cars between them. Traffic was bad, so they weren't moving that fast, and hopefully the man wasn't paying enough attention to the fact that he had a tail.

Out past Duarte, Asuza, and up out of the basin. At one point, Émile turned off, headed north, and Gunderson was afraid the man was going to drive all the way to the top of Mt. Baldy, but he turned into a neighborhood that the map on the front seat called San Antonio Heights, a little below the spot where the mountains started to go vertical.

Gunderson dropped back now, letting Émile have a big lead. If he'd been spotted, his target would either vanish now, or drive randomly to conceal his true destination and the rest of the evening would be a waste of time.

On the brighter side of things, the sun was low on the

horizon now, so Émile would be looking right at it in his rear-view mirror, while Gunderson could see clear to the mountains today, since there was just enough breeze to lift the smog and maybe push it towards Berdoo.

Émile turned up ahead onto a side street. Gunderson counted and turned two blocks short, running a little hot through a neighborhood, but there weren't any kids on bikes as he did, so he felt pretty safe.

Up one long block, Gunderson turned left and went one block closer to where Émile had turned, but still not on the same street before he turned right again and paralleled. Mostly just to make sure Émile hadn't done the same thing to lose a tail, like Gunderson occasionally did.

Clear, so he drove down another block and then cut over once more, but this time Gunderson came to a proper stop, like there might be a cop lurking nearby to write him a ticket it he rolled it. He looked both ways, but didn't see that four-door either direction. Not necessarily the worst outcome, as it hopefully meant that his target had gone to ground close by.

The road in front of him dead-ended at a brick wall, the kind that estates might put up around to keep the riffraff out. Gunderson grunted, feeling riffraffy today. That wall ran for several blocks either direction, like maybe someone had bought up a half-mile square at some point, so he turned right and puttered along.

His gut told him that was the place, but he'd gotten into too many scrapes over the years by rushing into things. Instead, he was intent on taking his time. Given the cover story about a Masonic Lodge dinner and meeting, he had a couple of hours before Émile would need to head home, at least according to the schedule Matilda Dubois had laid out for him.

Gunderson went to the end of the second block from

here before that brick wall ended at a corner, so he turned left again and followed it north as he and it went further up the hill. There was a mountain up there, and big, looping main road, so he knew that he'd be able to circle the enclosure. The only break in the wall was a solid door gate that looked like where a grounds crew would be able to open a padlock and access the interior, but the rest was brick, so he kept going for now. Sure enough, half-mile up and it turned again.

Just in case, Gunderson kept going straight and took the main road when he got there, turning left and following it around and down the hill until he got to the place Émile had turned originally. Traffic was light, but he wanted to see patterns, so he sat waiting to turn a few times where he probably could have made it. A car behind him honked a few times and then slipped into the other lane with a few choice profanities tossed his way.

The funniest part was when the man driving yelled at him to go back to Pasadena, where tonight's adventure had actually begun, but that was just the usual insult exchanged between Angelinos driving.

A couple of other expensive-looking cars turned in on this particular street, and they didn't fit the neighborhood. Gunderson's Mallory would be more at home, but he lived down in LA itself, rather than out in one of the new suburbs that were growing slowly together into a single, living entity.

After a red Brubaker turned, Gunderson slipped in behind it and then slowed some to let the car have space. Sure enough, down a block and a half it turned left into a driveway that had lights on.

Gunderson slowed as it turned then rolled past looking in. Lot of vehicles back there on a circular driveway in front of a large brick building, well-lit and looking like an old college campus. Totally out of place for the neighborhood, like it had been put in first and everything else later, maybe post-war.

Yeah, it felt like it had gone up in the Teens or Twenties, an older architecture than the new ranch houses across the street and around the campus.

Gunderson kept going, all the way down and then left up the hill to that one spot where he had seen the gate on the east side. He rolled past it slow, and found a spot along the curb where he could park, in between a flatbed truck and an old jalopy that looked to be about a '37. Cute, but even more battered and tired than the Mallory.

However, he didn't stick out here, and Émile's four-door would have. That was always the key to surveillance. Disappear into the setting and remain invisible to outsiders. Hopefully the locals won't take that much offense.

Gunderson parked and grabbed his hat and the camera bag off the seat as he got out. Weather was nice enough that he'd left the trench coat at home today, and he wasn't planning to be out to the wee hours when the basin got cold.

He looked both ways like a proper hoodlum crossing a busy street, even though it was empty, and then made his way to the gate. It was a little recessed from the brick wall itself, a space where a truck like the flatbed across the way could pull in out of traffic while the driver opened things up to get in.

Shiny padlock on a length of rusty chain kept it closed, about what he had expected. Still, nothing exotic, so he pulled out his wallet and extracted a couple of pieces of flattened steel he kept in there. Cops would recognize lockpicks, but not many other people.

He didn't bother kneeling down to look. Most of picking a lock was touch anyway, so he stood there and fiddled with it like he had the correct key and it was just being stubborn.

Not too stubborn, but it only had three pins, near as he

could tell without opening it up to check. Lock popped and he unthreaded the chain. Gunderson slipped the gate itself open enough to slip in and then rested the chain on it in such a way that it wouldn't swing the rest of the way, but would look maybe closed to a casual inspection.

Inside, it reminded him of an arboretum, more than anything. A big park of the sort that rich folks might fence off to keep riffraffy folk like Gunderson from enjoying themselves. Los Angeles had her share of those people, after all.

Trees way taller and greener than you normally got up here. Reminded him more of parts of Orange County where the groves stretched on forever, so he presumed a watering system of some sort. The grass on either side of the driveway he was on spoke to a well or something, pretty deep into the groundwater.

Lots of cover, which was probably both good and bad. He could sneak up on Émile and his friends, but someone else could get right on top of him in the evening gloom. Gunderson didn't figure dogs, since the front was open, unless there was a fence he'd missed.

Just in case, he reached down and touched the Smith & Wesson Model 29 under his arm in a shoulder rig. .44 Magnum, the modern upgrade from the .44 Special. Big gun. Lot tougher than the old .38 he'd worn as an MP or a cop before that. Pretty handy to shoot somebody as well, but in Gunderson's hands it made a perfectly serviceable sap.

Gunderson slipped off the driveway, mostly because it was gravel and he'd make noise walking. Onto the verge instead. It had been mowed recently enough that he wasn't wading through a jungle of crap to get where he was going.

Grounds were pretty damned flat in here. He could see a big brick building off in the distance. Again, looked more like a college campus than a house, but he couldn't remember any schools like that out in the neighborhood. Maybe Émile's friend just liked that architecture.

Three stories tall as he got closer. Probably a wide front coming back in two forks on the wings that enclosed a kind of Roman courtyard of a patio. No sounds, so they weren't having any sort of soirée on the patio tonight.

Good and bad. Let him get closer, but he'd probably have to break in to see anything, as opposed to sitting in the darkness with the camera in his bag taking pictures.

If old Émile was having an affair, he'd found himself a rich woman, which didn't feel right, so Gunderson kept moving on the assumption that maybe the guy was a spy after all.

Weirder things had happened around here, and the Rosenbergs hadn't been all that popular when the Feds killed them, not all that long ago.

Closer in, most of the building was dark. Or at least the sort of dim you got with room lights off and hallway light spilling in. Middle story was well lit, so he shifted around until he was pretty much lined up with the back of the building.

There was movement in a room there, but he couldn't get a good view. Fortunately, he had his camera bag with him, so Gunderson knelt down and swapped things around according to Clayton's notes, until he had the right lens for the range. Film was pretty good all around, because you never knew. He could always swap it for something else in a flash, but this would do, at least until he figured out what the next step was.

Gunderson found a spot with a good view and started dialing in the view-finder. Bunch of men in suits, standing around like a cocktail party or something. That pretty much scotched the whole idea of it being an affair, unless the whole thing was some sort of live porn show. But with a wife like

Matilda, why would any man go looking? Unless she was a special case, and he hadn't been hired for that sort of thing.

Gunderson got the focus and saw many men's faces, and not one woman. Again, about like the Lodge meeting the man was missing, but not. He snapped a couple of pictures, just on general principle, so he could have Clayton blow them up later and see if he recognized anybody.

Good enough. Gunderson shifted to his left a little to take some more pictures when he felt something hard prod him in the kidneys.

"Do not move, or I will be forced to hurt you," an oily voice whispered in his ear.

Or his neck, anyway. Fellow felt short compared to a tall Swede.

Crap.

Before Gunderson could do anything about the man, two more shadows detached themselves from the undergrowth and pointed guns at him.

"What do we do with him?" the first asked.

"Bring him inside," one of the others said. "We will let the Council decide."

Council? That didn't sound like fun, but there wasn't a lot Gunderson could do about it right now.

He let them direct him forward after one took his camera and his bag. They hadn't found his revolver. Hadn't even looked for it, but the things they were pointing at him sure didn't look like automatics, either. More like Buck Rogers-style ray guns.

What the hell was going on?

THEY ENDED up hustling him into the building pretty quickly. Three men covered him with things that looked like pistols from a Saturday morning pulp serial, but they seemed serious and Gunderson didn't feel like finding out the truth personally.

He ended up in a library. Lot of foot traffic on the hardwood floor outside, all of it receding, so Gunderson assumed that he'd spooked the crowd. Amateur move on his part, but how the hell had they found him in the darkness so easily? Or snuck up on him?

Gunderson knew he'd been perfectly silent. Occupational requirement in this field.

Two of the goons had kept him covered. Both middle-aged looking fellows. Maybe half a foot shorter than him. Looked vaguely Slavic, but no accent he'd been able to detect. Off-the-rack suits expertly tailored, dark green and mud brown respectively. Neither wore glasses.

Come to think of it, none of the men in the view-finder had worn glasses, which was just weird. Especially as the age of the men had ranged from mid-thirties to mid-sixties, from external appearances.

And none of them wore glasses?

Émile didn't, but Gunderson hadn't marked that as special at the time. He wasn't sure now why it stood out, but it was rare in this business. Unless you were in Hollywood, and then folks took them off when the camera rolled and put them back on afterwards.

Émile entered now, along with four other older men and a couple more goons.

Gunderson was on a couch, sitting in the middle. Nice couch. Nice room. Built-in bookcases filled with spines and artwork that looked tasteful. Man's kind of room, done in dark cherry polished down, with throw rugs over hardwood. Couple of suits of Spanish armor on stands in the corners. A few portraits that felt more like they'd been here when the current owner moved in, whoever he was.

Except that the building wasn't that old. Nothing in Los Angeles was. Hell, Pasadena used to be the cattle pens of the Patton family, according to the stories he'd been told.

Émile pulled a chair around to face him. Two of the other men did as well, while the other two stood on the wings. And four men with ray guns pointing at him, in case Gunderson was feeling frisky.

"Eugene Gunderson," Émile announced, although he should have no idea unless Matilda had set him up. "We located your car and read your registration."

Oh you did, did you?

"That's correct," he agreed. Man hadn't asked a question yet.

"Did you check to see if he was armed?" Émile asked one of the guards.

"We did not," the man answered, crestfallen.

Gunderson nodded.

"Shoulder holster, left side," he said. "License is in my outside breast pocket."

Both got taken pretty fast, but not especially professionally.

"You are a private investigator, Mr. Gunderson?" Émile asked.

"That's correct."

"Who are you investigating, Mr. Gunderson?"

"You, Mr. Dubois," Gunderson replied.

Not like he had a lot of latitude right now, with four ray guns trained on him and nine men. Not even remotely a fair fight, but he hadn't done anything except trespassing so far. Grounds for a good talking to by the Sheriff, but that was about it. And the man didn't have any reason to hate Gunderson.

The Sheriff, that is. He had no idea about Émile.

Still, his words were like a big rock dropped in a small pond from the way everyone recoiled.

Except Émile.

Telling, that.

"I was hired by Mrs. Dubois," Gunderson continued, aware that he was walking a fine line, but none of this set up felt right. "She had suspicions about you and asked me to look."

More noise. Mostly inarticulate grumblings and gasps, but they settled pretty quickly.

"She did not suspect me of having an affair?" Émile asked sardonically.

"You've met the woman," Gunderson countered. "Even in L.A., I'd be hard pressed to find a more beautiful one. Don't know that much about her personality."

"Brilliant, Mr. Gunderson," Émile said. "That beauty is matched by a first-rate mind. She would have made an exceptional actor, but that almost requires being struck by lightning in this town."

"So she found a rich, French industrialist with a few secrets instead and was happy enough?" Gunderson asked.

"So it seemed," the man nodded. "But apparently not."

"What is this Council that man mentioned?" Gunderson nodded at the closest goon, just to watch the man blush and stammer.

That finally got through to the man. Émile moued with his mouth, as though he had just sucked a lemon. The other grumbled louder now, but he waved them to silence.

"What has she told you, Mr. Gunderson?" he asked.

"How were you able to locate my car so quickly?" he fired right back. "And track me in the shadows or move so silently that I never saw any of you coming?"

More noise. Soft spot in the armor, apparently, over a sensitive bit, to see the faces around him blanch.

"Mr. Gunderson, you are dealing with things that may be larger than you imagine," Émile began, but Gunderson interrupted him.

Useful, watching them stagger from thought to thought as he stymied them.

"She's of the opinion that you're a Commie spy, Émile," Gunderson snapped at the man, but he was watching the others react. The junior varsity players, as it were. "That's what she's telling people, anyway."

Okay, technically a lie. She'd only told one person that Gunderson was aware of, but he was outnumbered nine to one right now, so blowing things up would maybe protect him.

Too easy to make Gunderson just disappear, if they were that good. He wanted to make them work for it.

Riot, first class.

Émile actually had to stand up and wave his hands to get their attention over the inchoate yammering.

"QUIET!" he snarled over the voices.

Finally, he got everyone calmed down, but Gunderson had seen enough.

The looks of surprise had given way to angry denial, rather than embarrassment or deception.

Émile scowled at him now. Gunderson studied the man closer in turn.

Fifty, give or take. Well founded and well kept. Well-dressed in a bespoke suit that fit perfectly, navy blue with razor-thin pinstripes. Full head of hair leaning towards leonine and starting to gray in such a way that was natural, rather than dye wearing off. Brown eyes and a clipped mustache dominated a strong face.

Soft hands was the only weak part about the man that Gunderson could find.

"Communist spy?" the man asked, his voice still containing traces of incredulous.

"Russian, Chinese, or CPA, she wasn't entirely clear," Gunderson replied. "McCarthy might have finally been shut down, but there are still folks out there willing to blow on those coals again, if they thought they might find something."

"And how do you feel about that, Mr. Gunderson?" Émile asked.

"Figure she's a smart woman, Émile," he said. "If she wanted to destroy you, all it would take was a phone call to the local newspaper or maybe some Congressman. She struck me as a concerned spouse, rather than a vengeful one. You still haven't answered my first question."

"Yes, I have not," Émile nodded. He sat back in his chair and actually crossed his legs before gesturing at the other four men. "We are The Council, Mr. Gunderson."

Gunderson nodded. He'd already sorted everyone out. Four dwarves led by a Chairman, seated across from him. Four goons with ray guns, for all they were dressed for a semi-formal cocktail party.

And Émile didn't strike him as a killer. None of them did, even the punks with guns. Helped that California kept the gas chamber warm these days.

Gunderson watched the man control his minions with charisma alone. Impressive feat.

"Communism is a phase, Mr. Gunderson," Émile began.

"Just Gunderson," he said. Felt like they were letting their hair down, maybe.

"Gunderson," Émile nodded. "Capitalism is also just a phase, as was monarchism, feudalism, or colonialism."

"Lot of *-isms* in your world, Dubois," Gunderson noted.

"Your world, Gunderson," Émile smiled. "We are just visitors here."

Gunderson chewed on that. Didn't feel like he meant folks from France when he said it like that. Not with the Buck Rogers gear. Or all these men and nobody wearing glasses.

Lots of clues that something just wasn't right here.

"I don't really want to know where you're really from, do I?" he asked obliquely.

Émile smiled. The others blanched, but they were all junior varsity, weren't they?

"Quite possibly no," Émile said. "How do I convince you I am not a threat, Gunderson?"

"Don't see you are a threat, Dubois," he said. "But I was hired because your wife is concerned that you might embarrass her and ruin her social standing and possibly get her knocked back down into a farm girl from Indiana. You know, commie spy and all that."

Émile *considered* things for a moment. That was the look on his face.

"You are a private investigator, Gunderson," he finally said. "A man who can keep secrets when he needs to?"

"That's right," Gunderson agreed. "My job requires a man people can trust with their secrets. I lose that reputation and I might as well go back to being a line cook."

"So I could show you something that should convince you I am not a communist, Gunderson," Émile smiled. "That we are not Russian or Chinese agents."

"You didn't say you weren't a spy," Gunderson pointed out.

"That's because I don't want to lie to you, Mr. Gunderson," Émile said simply. "We are spies, but not for those nations or peoples."

"Who, then?"

"We come from much farther away."

Gunderson had a sinking feeling, but he nodded.

After all, if he'd wanted a boring life, he could have gone back to Seattle and been a cop after the war.

"Then what?" he asked.

"My wife hired you to determine that I was not a communist spy, correct?" Émile asked. "Specifically that?"

"Specifically that, yes," Gunderson agreed.

This was going to be one of those days where *technically* correct was the best kind, but Gunderson felt like he'd stepped deep in the shit this time.

"And you are a man who prides himself on being able to keep secrets, yes?"

"That's right," Gunderson agreed, maybe a little sourly.

Émile rose now and gestured Gunderson to do the same.

"Are you sure this is wise?" the man on the left asked in a concerned voice.

"I find it necessary," Émile replied before turning to face Gunderson. "And we will have people watching you after this, to insure that you keep your promise of silence, Gunderson."

That was it. Nothing more.

For a man three inches shorter and maybe thirty pounds lighter, it came across as a most effective threat. The calm, measured delivery helped.

Gunderson had been threatened by professionals in his time. Émile Dubois could probably give them all lessons.

"Come," Émile turned towards the door. "This way."

Gunderson fell into line behind the man, surrounded by goons and accountants.

Down they went, into the first basement and through a door that had been expertly concealed to reveal another staircase, down another level.

At least.

The Buck Rogers/Flash Gordon feel of things suddenly

made more sense as he followed Émile through another door and into a…what?

Gunderson might have called it a motor pool, after his days in the army being an MP, when he'd really wanted to get into Armor instead. But he couldn't identify any of the vehicles in here.

If they were vehicles.

He'd been to the Saturday matinee a few times, still up or up early. He'd seen the bad B-rated films with flying saucers and monsters from space, usually just cheap special effects and makeup.

The thing dominating the room might have been a flying saucer, except that it didn't glow. Not right now, anyway. Something on the right looked like an Indian motorcycle, except that it didn't have wheels, with spoilers like the back of an old P-38 on the front forks.

He turned to find Émile smiling at him, rather knowingly.

"Socialism is your future as a species, if you successfully navigate the current age, Gunderson," the man said grandly. "Not Communism as Lenin, Stalin, Mao, or the other fools might have expressed it. That is just totalitarianism with a different hat. Think of where Germany or the Nordic countries are headed for a much better example."

Gunderson chewed on the inside of his cheek for a moment.

"Okay, I gotta ask," he said. "Where are you people from?"

"If Earth is at galactic south on a projection, roughly three-quarters of the way out from the Galactic Core, we come from a planet ninety-seven of your light-years north-by-northwest up the Orion Arm."

Every one of those words sounded like they were English,

but none of them made a damned bit of sense to Gunderson. Still, he nodded and studied Émile.

"And you can't have children because you aren't really human, right?" he asked, starting to understand.

"That is correct," the man nodded. "One of the great disappointments of my career, too, because she is such an amazing woman. I occasionally wonder if she should have an affair outside our marriage, just so she can have a child, but it is not a topic I would broach with her."

Gunderson nodded back.

"Is it acceptable if I tell her you work for some secret, government research institute or something?" he asked the man, including the others in his gaze. "Woman that smart needs something to keep her from worrying."

"That would be acceptable, Gunderson," Émile agreed. "And in a year or so, perhaps I will be able to share more details with her."

"Then I've seen what I need to see," Gunderson said. "If someone can open my camera and destroy that roll of film, I have no evidence of the rest of you for anyone to blackmail you later."

"It has already been done," Émile said. "Come, your car awaits upstairs."

Gunderson followed the man out the front door to find his '49 Mallory parked in the driveway, instead of where he'd left it. He still had the keys in his pocket, but Gunderson supposed that aliens might be able to hotwire an old heap like that without damaging anything.

He found the camera bag, revolver, and ID in the front seat when Émile escorted him over, the rest remaining up on the porch and just watching nervously.

"I don't get you," Gunderson said to the man when they were alone.

Émile smiled sadly and cocked his head to the left.

"That is understandable, Gunderson," he replied. "Our mission is to try to save humanity, from itself, as well as from others."

"Others," he repeated.

"Do you think all the strange things that have happened since the Second World War are the result of local technology and developments? No, you have come to the attention of many players out there. Most are neutral. A few, like myself and my comrades, support you. Others would see harm done, fearing what humans might be like if they escaped this world at their present stage of development."

"Where do I fit in all that?" Gunderson asked.

"You have the hardest job of all as a private detective, Gunderson," Émile said. "You are *The Man Who Knows*, but you have already taken it upon yourself to bring order from chaos, so we are not all that different, you and I."

Gunderson didn't have a handy retort to that, so he got in the Mallory and turned the engine over to a rumbly purr.

"My mechanic suggests that you are losing your number three spark plug," Émile said over the sound. "I can recommend a shop."

Gunderson nodded and slipped it into gear, letting the engine cover any thing he might have said.

Wasn't a lot to say. He did indeed know too much about this town, but that was a hazard of the job.

His job was to protect it. Or rather, the weak who were prey for the strong.

So maybe he and Émile Dubois had that much in common.

FATALE

THE GUNDERSON CASE FILES (003)
FATALE

GUNDERSON HAD ALWAYS FIGURED that *femme fatale* was more a Hollywood thing than a reality in the private detective business. Even in Los Angeles. Sure, he'd met his share of dangerous dames in his line of trade, but most of them were the kind that *got* you killed rather than doing the killing themselves. Still, he was wondering if he'd finally met one this time.

The envelope with the instructions had arrived with money. Expenses for a day-hire. Directions to arrive at this address and ask for *Madame al-Taghut*. He had and had done.

From the outside, the building had looked like any other house, north outside L.A. itself, up and over in the Valley. Money, but still a ranch like all the post-war craze. Bigger than a bungalow, but not a mansion like you maybe found over in Pasadena.

Big, but they all were in this neighborhood. Quaint, well-maintained, fitting in well with the neighbors. A quiet maid had met him at the door and listened to his spiel before inviting him in and asking him to wait in what felt more like the front room of a doctor's office than a living room. Two tan, leather couches that were okay now but probably turned into torture in the summer heat that was coming in a few months. A coffee table in front of both. There was a thing about the size of a cigar box that looked like one of those cheap Egyptian mummy cases the Pharaohs were supposedly buried in. Sarcophagus, that was the word,

The art on the walls was Middle Eastern in nature, but owed more to the Hollywood image of sheikhs and kasbahs than reality, like someone with a copy of *A Thousand and One Nights* and a decorating budget had been turned loose. Sheer silk cloth hangings over two walls just to make it feel like the inside of a tent. Paintings as well as Ansel Adams-style photos of camels and bedouins.

Gunderson had sat and made peace with whatever weird shit this case might promise, if only because they'd already given him cash up front for one day of his life and expenses to drive up here, regardless of whether or not he took the case.

Then she walked in.

Sashayed, perhaps. Something.

He'd have liked to say she was dressed, but Gunderson would have been lying in just about any jurisdiction that wanted him under oath. Sure, she was wearing something, but it didn't cover anything.

Gunderson supposed you could call it a robe of a type that a woman might wear when emerging from her bath, but it was so thin as to be basically transparent. And there was nothing under it but woman.

And she was woman, as close as he was willing to look. The robe was tied in a manner that might suggest negligence to the uninformed, except that the lapels were more or less hooked on firm, hanging breasts that reminded Gunderson of torpedoes going into the water.

Below that…

Her personal grooming standards were better than his, as she had apparently shaved everything he could see, which was everything. In its place, someone had left a tattoo. He hoped it was a tattoo, as Gunderson couldn't remember ever encountering a henna that black. Any other suggestions were too weird to contemplate.

It was an octopus, belled head upright between her sex and her navel, right where her belly bulged out a little into a rim. Intelligent eyes that just about lined up with the top ends of her uterus, if he had the anatomy correct. Two small, upright tentacles bracketed her belly button, while the other six, arms and suckers, flashed out over both hip bones and down the fronts of her thighs.

The beast's beak was left to the imagination, if it actually took any to envision.

Gunderson worked his way north again, having seen what she wanted him to see first. The face seemed young, but the neck and hands told different stories. Those suggested a woman older than him, somewhere in a well-preserved forties under a layer of makeup designed to obscure. The hair was black with just a few gray roots visible under a decent dye job.

"Madame al-Taghut?" he asked politely. Hey, she'd paid for the privilege of showing herself off to him today.

The name suggested Egypt or at least the southeastern Mediterranean Sea. Possibly further inland. But for the name, he might have guessed her to be half-Mexican. A little darker than the Hispanics in this town, but not as much red to her skin.

The shell was certainly impressively beautiful, but that just suggested all the ugliness was underneath, out of sight for the moment.

"Do you like what you see?" she asked in a breathless

voice that all the young girls practiced when they wanted to go to Hollywood. "Or does it frighten you?"

Gunderson shrugged.

"There's a girl in Tijuana who got a similar tattoo, only hers was a great white shark coming right at you with her black hair for a mouth," he said in an offhand manner. "So realistic that she had to learn to give really good handjobs, in order to stay in business."

The eyes flashed hot hatred for a second, but that was fine. If she really wanted to hire him for a case, her rate had just gone up anyway, since his tolerance for bullshit was pretty much already at quota before he'd walked in here. He smiled up at her and dared her to push the woman luck. He had most of a foot and a hundred pounds on Madame al-Taghut if she was feeling frisky.

Something must have been there in his eyes, because she sat on a different couch, around the corner from him where a fan might swirl the spring air enough to be chilly on a day like this. Thankfully, she didn't cross her legs, nor turn her sex towards him in such a way as to threaten him with her beak.

She studied him again for a long moment, before reaching out one hand to reveal that the sarcophagus held cheap Turkish cigarettes and a lighter. That was good, as he didn't feel like getting close enough to offer her a light right now.

She lit and puffed a few times, thankfully blowing the smoke away from him while he still had a few nerves left for her to get on.

Nobody was ever going to outwait Gunderson. Too many years of stakeouts and tailing people. Thankfully, he wasn't feeling the itch to smoke today, so he didn't need to root around inside her box for his daily pleasure.

"You're a cool one," she finally offered.

The voice said *femme fatale*, right out of the movies. Those B-flicks running at the cheap theaters where you can walk in midway and just watch through to the middle of the next showing and not be lost at any point. Gunderson smiled at her. It wasn't a particularly pleasant smile, but she didn't strike him as a particularly pleasant woman.

And there was always Tijuana if he felt the urge.

"You come highly recommended," she tried another tack when he didn't bite.

Not yet, anyway. He might still bite.

"Oh?" Gunderson finally offered her a nibble of his own.

"Joyce suggested that you were the right man for my needs," she continued.

Joyce had, had she?

Gunderson wondered about Joyce's friends sometimes. His friend was an old Hollywood starlet from the early days who had never quite made it past chorus girl. Joyce had ended up marrying shady money instead, and then inheriting it all when some of her first husband's other gangster friends killed him.

Gunderson didn't bother suppressing his derisive snort at this Egyptian woman. Considered just walking out right now and saving everyone the time and energy of dancing around the topic until dinner time. He could be home for a late lunch if traffic wasn't too bad.

"Not that way," she said, suddenly blushing hard, with absolutely nothing to cover it as he watched the flood of red creep down her torso.

They say that the blush is the one thing that nobody can fake. If so, at least there was something honest about the woman.

"I mean to hire you to locate something for me," she said.

Gunderson nodded ambivalently, presuming that her virginity was long past the statute of limitations at this point.

"Joyce tells me that you tend to specialize in cases beyond the usual stock and trade for a private detective in this city," she said, letting everything just hang at that point, in case he wanted a bite after all.

Maybe. Beautiful woman offering, and all that.

"I have a higher pain threshold for the weird and stupid than most of my peers, perhaps," Gunderson finally gave her an opening.

This case already felt like it was going to be going to the stranger side. Might as well short-cut it.

"There is a book," Madame al-Taghut finally got serious now, holding out her hands to frame something Gunderson figured would be filed in the library under folios. Maybe eighteen wide and twenty-six tall. From the way she was holding her hands, somewhere around four inches thick, too.

Must be heavy. And probably weird if Joyce had sent this woman to him.

"Okay?" he went ahead and asked.

T&A notwithstanding, she had paid for his time.

"We believe that it is in the possession of Daniel van Gelder right now," she said.

Oh, him.

Gunderson scowled, but it was at a punk like van Gelder, and not this beautiful woman.

"You are familiar with this person?" she asked, hopeful.

Gunderson was picking up hints of accent now as she spoke. Like maybe everything up to now had been a set piece she had worked out ahead of time and was now having to think on her feet. Sounded Arabic with hints of something else under it. You ran into just about every language on Earth, somewhere in Los Angeles, if you were patient.

"I am," Gunderson said. "Less polite people might refer

to him as a pimp, as he deals in flesh in this town, connecting young starlets just off the bus with…older gentlemen who might be interested in making a trade, shall we say?"

It was her turn to nod.

Yeah, Gunderson knew that punk. Had been hired not that long ago by a couple of worried parents from Peoria, Illinois wanting to locate their daughter and help her escape whatever she had fallen into. Hadn't taken much. Bus fare, a few extra bucks for food, and a metaphorical kick in the pants to get Becky to see that her and that girl from Tijuana were mostly separated by geography, not occupation.

"Why's a punk like him want a special book?" he asked.

"It is more than a book," the woman turned serious now.

She seemed to age before his eyes. Still beautiful beyond measure, but less Mother and more Crone now, except that she wasn't Celtic by any stretch of the imagination. Still, the Morrigan would have claimed this woman as one of hers if asked.

"Joyce tells me that you are a man of your word, Mr. Gunderson," she said.

He nodded, short and sharp. Man didn't have much in this world beyond that. And you never owned anything that you couldn't carry with you at a dead run while being chased.

"You will forgive me for testing you then," she continued. *Maybe, lady. Only maybe.*

"I wanted to see if you were the sort of man who wouldn't immediately fall all over himself when offered pleasures, carnal or otherwise," al-Taghut said "The book is a threat to everything and everyone on this planet."

"Is that so?" Gunderson asked.

With any other woman, it would have come out sarcastic and rude, but they'd already started dancing, at least verbally.

Gone somewhere on the far side of serious just in the last thirty seconds.

"It is a living being, if you wish to look on such a thing with eyes that can see beyond this mortal realm," she more or less growled at him now, looking less beautiful and more deadly with each syllable. "It will make you promises, for those foolish enough to listen."

"Huh," Gunderson grunted back at her. "What's the pimp want?"

"Who can say?" she replied, waving a hand negligently in the air. The one with the cigarette, so it swished smoke everywhere. "Power. Wealth. Eternal life."

"Sounds like a trap," he opined.

"They always are," she nodded, back to just beautiful and deadly now. "The book was stolen from my organization a generation ago, and we have been hunting it since 1924. A chance remark fell on the right ears and we were able to send someone to America to investigate."

"You," Gunderson guessed.

She nodded.

"Got no backup?" he asked now.

"Only contacts," al-Taghut said. "We are a small group of scholars, dedicated to protecting such knowledge and keeping it from being used for evil."

"Eternal life?" he asked, taking the time to ogle the woman from head to toe in a most obvious manner. Not that it was that great a chore.

"Perhaps not eternal, but greatly extended," she replied now. "But in the wrong hands, fools might dabble in powers far beyond their imagination, or even unleash the destruction of the world."

There were things she wasn't telling him, but Gunderson wasn't surprised by that. Some days, he wondered if there was some sort of bizarre gravitational field that caused all the weirdness in the world to flow downhill into the Los Angeles basin. Somewhere close to where he had an office.

Crap like this had never happened when he was a cop or a detective up in Seattle. But that was before the war, and Hitler had stirred up some things before he'd been taken down. Gunderson wondered how long it would be until everything settled down again.

If it did.

"And if I happen to find this book?" he asked. "Then what?"

Again, those eyes flared with something he could only describe as pure evil. Or need. He'd seen a few hopheads going through withdrawal that had a similar gleam.

"You will return it to me for payment, and I will vanish with it forever," she said, at least giving him something honest now.

Gunderson wasn't willing to believe in that body. Even when she was showing him damned near everything. Or maybe because of that. Most women had something to hide, after all. Makeup, hair dye, girdles, or hose.

Gunderson gave her a good dose of cop eye now. He'd only been a detective from '40 until early '42, but he'd been a cop for six years before that and three with the army afterwards. And a PI for a couple of years in LA now.

"What's your flavor of evil?" he asked.

Gunderson didn't really care. Money was money, and if he was laundering something achieved through evil, at least he was putting it to a righteous use. And Joyce had apparently sent her.

Damned if she didn't lick her lips as she smiled at him. Even did that little lip bite thing.

"I have no interest in summoning the Old Ones to destroy this world," she said.

"And you think van Gelder might?" Gunderson asked, mostly to be sure but clueless as to what it might mean.

She hadn't answered his question, so much as drawn a not-past-here kind of line in the sand with it.

"We have no idea what he might do with access to that kind of power," Madame al-Taghut replied. "It will not be the benefit of Humanity, whatever it is."

No, Gunderson didn't figure that punk would.

So, she was being evasive, but he didn't get the feeling that those tentacles were going to reach out and drag him to his death, at least not until he made the mistake of getting too close to them. Everybody's gotta die, but he'd rather put it off for a while yet, even as beautiful as she was.

"All right," he said. "Joyce wouldn't send you to me unless you had convinced her, and that's no easy task. Might charge a little extra, just because I'm going to need to bribe a few librarians along the way."

"They won't recognize the book, even if you placed it before them," she said, still licking her lips with anticipation of…something.

"No, but they'll hear about stolen books in this town and can help save me time and you money," he countered.

"Money is irrelevant," she said with such casual disdain that he knew she wasn't kidding.

So this was something that even money could not buy, apparently.

They settled on a rate and she paid him for a week up front. Cash. Big bills. Crisp ones that she had gotten from the kind of bank that had a coat of arms carved into the stone lintel out front.

Gunderson found himself headed back over the hills, down into LA proper. Lunch would be a little late, but not that much.

Then he'd be getting himself into the book business.

GUNDERSON CLIMBED the sidewalk slowly up three sets of short steps that got you to the massive mansion. The monstrosity was set well back from the street and up on a hill, the kind that had apparently been created for the purpose of letting it be taller than all its neighbors, who hadn't envisioned the need until an asshole had moved in.

But then, most of them probably didn't put lifts in their shoes, either.

The area screamed *stately.* All these mansions with their manicured yards and Japanese gardeners, but most of those homeowners were merely wealthy. Bankers and shippers, for the most part. Hollywood money went further west up the coast or into the hills, when it wanted to escape the prying eyes and outstretched palms of the vice squad.

The sun was barely past zenith, headed into that long, quiet afternoon of the spring when the basin was still pleasant and the trees were just starting to flower with anticipation.

Daniel van Gelder needed to be close to Hollywood. Physically as well as metaphorically, like a parasite that couldn't be away from its host for too long or it would die. Except that Gunderson supposed that van Gelder probably filled the roll of a remora better these days, catching all the tidbits lost by a voracious shark as it fed on everything that came along.

Yes, that man could be discriminating. After all, the shark was offered a buffet of hundreds of young men and women every year, and only needed dozens. The rest had to find jobs, and there were only so many places a beautiful, nubile, young woman could waitress while she waited to be discovered.

Gunderson reached the porch finally, not winded but

annoyed. This space was just as much a statement as everything else, being big enough to tuck a small orchestra off to one side, if you needed such a thing to serenade guests arriving.

He approached the enormous double doors, done in the Napoleonic style, fourteen feet tall, and considered the wrought iron knocker that looked like a dragon's head and tongue. He settled for the buzzer to one side, since he didn't know where that knocker had been, or the last person to use it.

There was just enough feedback to let him know that the bell was ringing inside, so Gunderson let go and stepped back. He had worn a nicer suit today, recently pressed and everything, dark brown and muted in a way that didn't suggest he was a reporter out to cause trouble.

Trouble, sure. Just not the kind that made the evening papers.

He went ahead and removed his fedora, holding it in his off hand like the kind of gentleman who expected to immediately be invited in. Longshot, but possible.

The doors split open like an octopus showing you its tongue. A butler stood in the opening, guarding it well, as Gunderson could see where he had braced a boot behind the door, just in case someone gave him the bums rush.

"Yes?" the man asked in a deep Atlantic accent that was as cultivated as the suit. And as fake.

But we're all just players, aren't we? And everything is a stage. The Bard had said that, one of the few things Gunderson agreed wholeheartedly with.

He handed the man his business card. The nice ones that went to folks with money.

"I would like to call on Mr. van Gelder for a few minutes," Gunderson said with a shiny, useless smile. "I don't have an appointment, but presumed that it would be better if I came here before I went to talk to Lt. Kowalski downtown."

That would be *Head of LAPD Homicide Lt. Kowalski.*

Gunderson stepped back and smiled at the big bruiser in the fancy suit. Got the door closed in his face, which was fine. Gave him a chance to study the surroundings.

Fancy, but in a *nouveau riche* kind of way that Fitzgerald might have recognized. But most of Los Angeles was that way. Unless you had connections to the Pattons or one of the other old ranching families, you were just a newcomer trying to get rich. Or famous. Sometimes both, if you got lucky.

van Gelder had supposedly approached it sideways, seeing a market niche and quietly fulfilling it. The house felt more like a movie set than an abode. False front hiding all manner of rough ugliness on the inside. Rather like Madame al-Taghut, but she was paying him enough to not mind. Or at least not comment out loud.

Eventually, the door opened again and Gunderson got ushered inside. Past the sitting room just past the coat closet. Beyond the grand staircase that dominated a foyer designed to have a grand staircase to show off.

The butler walked quieter than most of the people Gunderson had ever met, even with boots on. Fellow had to check over a shoulder occasionally to make sure Gunderson was still behind him. At the same time, Gunderson was used to stalking right up to open windows to get the photograph he needed to make his case. Or his conviction.

They ended up on the back patio. The fake hill had been put to good use here, with an enormous swimming pool surrounded by stonework and a few plants that mostly just gave the place character.

Must have hired someone better this time, or maybe he did all his seductions here, so this was the front of the set, rather than the back.

It was Hollywood. Everyone understood camera angles and lighting.

There were a trio of bathing beauties, one swimming and two laying in the sun. Matched set, even, with a blond, a brunette, and a redhead.

Daniel van Gelder sat at an outdoor table made of wrought iron, under an unnecessary umbrella, with what appeared to be a rum cocktail in one hand and a telephone headset in the other. He looked up as Gunderson came into view and his demeanor changed with a quick shiver.

"Hey, I'll call you back in a bit," the man said. "Got an unexpected visitor. 'kay."

He hung up and Gunderson studied him. After lunch and the man was still wearing silk pajamas, with a silk-looking robe over them, tied at the waist but open.

The butler led him close and then stepped off to one side. About where Gunderson would want to stand if he was about to sap someone, so Gunderson smiled up at him. Tall fellow. Long, ape-like arms.

Gunderson had learned a few things in Seattle and had practiced them on grunts in Africa and Europe.

"What do you want, shamus?" van Gelder asked bluntly before taking a goodly-sized drink.

The glow in his eyes and face suggested that this wasn't even his second glass today. But Gunderson knew how to time things like this.

Gunderson turned to watch the bevy of young women. They had almost as much exposed flesh as the Egyptian woman, but none of it was nearly as well organized. Nor any visible ink. He turned back to van Gelder.

"Given the nature of the questions I was hoping you might be able to assist with, maybe we should head indoors?" he asked innocently. "Fewer witnesses. Got a library or something where we might talk?"

Heavy scowl. Like maybe the man was already a little too drunk to walk normally and didn't want to the world knowing it. Gunderson smiled like a PI getting ready to put a pimp's feet to the fire.

"Yeah, sure," he said, turning to the ape. "Put him in the library. I'll be along shortly."

Gunderson nodded as the butler headed back indoors, trailing him a little more noisily now, just to keep the peace.

"You will wait here," the butler instructed him from the door, closing it and leaving Gunderson alone.

Library. Nice place. Must have been another set, the kind you used when you had a cute, little intellectual on your hands, instead of the usual farm-girl who was dumber than a mud fence post, which was most of them. Lots of books, all leather bound and expensively done. A little more dust than one might expect, but not enough to suggest van Gelder never came in here.

Portrait of the homeowner as a Roman Emperor on one wall. As a bullfighter on another. Arthurian knight on a third. All of them painted to look taller than Gunderson's six-foot-three, which was no surprise, as he'd caught van Gelder in slippers on the patio.

Crossing his hands behind his back, Gunderson wandered around, mostly looking at the curios the man had collected. A lot of it was junk, but one whole side of the room had an Egyptian flavor, probably from all that ruckus when Carter and Carvnarvon found that Pharoah in Egypt in '22. Madame al-Taghut had said the book had vanished in '24.

The thing that caught his attention was a leather-bound folio, resting closed on a reading lectern. Smelled old. With a hint of brimstone. Maybe the dust you found in an Egyptian tomb, except that this one had been opened a lot earlier than the one found by Carter and his friends.

Gunderson carefully lifted the front cover just enough to peek at the first page, but not open it. The swirl inked inside was an octopus, nearly identical to what Madame al-Taghut had on her lower belly, so he closed it again and slipped into the chair across from a small desk where van Gelder might pretend to interview some pretty thing, before leading her over the oversized monstrosity on one side that screamed casting couch, as out of place as it was to the rest of the furniture in here.

But then, Gunderson already knew what sorts of services van Gelder allegedly provided to the old money in this town. Nothing had ever been proven, of course, and all investigations were quashed so quickly that they might make your head spin.

However, if Gunderson's next step was Kowalski downtown, that was a button that was actually connected. After all, Kowalski wasn't Vice. He was Homicide. That suggested a dead girl, which was always one of the two best ways you got a scandal in this town.

van Gelder slimed his way into the room on unsteady feet. Gunderson pretended to ignore the man until he made it to the chair. Bruiser was again in the right spot to swing a sap. Gunderson wondered if he'd end up having to shoot the dumb bastard, one of these days.

"All right, we're here, and away from the girls," the pimp groused, still holding a tall glass with ice, juice, and enough rum that it was oozing from the man's pores right now. "What's so damned important?"

Luckily, Gunderson read every newspaper that came out. You needed to know what was printed, as well as what the powers in this town didn't allow on paper. Plus, he talked to people. Big, small, white, brown, red, yellow. Made no difference in his line of work.

So Gunderson spun a believable-enough tale of a missing

girl. Young, pretty, filled with all those dreams. Mentioned Montana this time, instead of someplace more cosmopolitan, as a Montana girl would stick out like a sore thumb.

But she'd vanished. Gone, like she never existed outside Gunderson's fertile imagination and facile tongue. He'd been hired by the parents to find her, but every lead had turned up empty.

Did Daniel van Gelder maybe have any leads on a missing rancher's daughter?

As stories went, these kinds of things were a dime a dozen in this town. Gunderson had made it a point to describe her in a manner similar to the younger version of Madame al-Taghut that he saw in his mind, as white girls with black hair were pretty rare naturally. He left out the interesting bits of the physical description, assuming that this punk would know about that tattoo.

Finally, Gunderson wound himself down to a stuttering, flailing whatever, like he'd run out of words. He looked at the pimp of Hollywood with an expectant face.

"Yer barkin' up the wrong tree here, Gunderson," the man snapped. "Never seen her before, nor even heard anything like it. They sure she even made it this far? Lots of girls like that stop midway and maybe fall into bad things, you know."

Gunderson nodded sagely, defeated. The lucky ones only made it as far as Sacramento or Denver, where they had to get a job doing menial stuff, but at least got to keep their clothes on. The unlucky ones sat in this same chair and had different conversations with drunk casting directors who had handy couches.

Gunderson shook his head in defeat. He grimaced. Everything he could do to convince this man that he had nothing to fear.

"Guess I'll try my luck elsewhere then," he said, rising carefully as he watched the ape out of the corner of his eye.

"I got your card," van Gelder sneered. "If she wanders in, I'll let you know when I'm done with her."

Gunderson almost took a poke at the guy for that, but held himself still. He couldn't save them all. Or even a fraction. No one could.

He just had to hold the line at his end of things and let the rest of the world go to hell without him.

Bruiser saw him out without a world, glowering triumphantly as he did, like they'd all pulled a fast one on him.

Gunderson got himself into the front seat of his old '49 Mallory and sucked down a hard breath. Right about now, a cigarette might have been worth it, but he wanted to stop and you didn't cut corners in this business. Didn't start making excuses, or you'd just keep on at it until one day you were done.

Gunderson wasn't done. Not by a long shot.

But then, he already knew that this case wasn't, either.

LIKE HE'D BEEN WARNED, the woman at the University Library couldn't tell Gunderson anything about the book, even after he'd described it.

"Got anything I might read about for background?" Gunderson tried a new tack.

The woman just stared at him for several moments. He guessed her to be in her fifties, so about fifteen years older than he was. Fortunately, there was a ring on her hand proclaiming that she was married.

He didn't ask about the happily part, as she was a lot too frumpy and a little too heavy for his tastes, or he might have considered her look to be in invitation to a seduction. It happened, occasionally. Folks who had seen all the movies and had this grand expectation that PI work was something other than gritty and tedious. Apes with saps were far more common in his line of work than beautiful dames or libraries.

Gunderson slipped her a fin and watched the woman's eyes grow big.

"I'm on a strange case and my expenses include bribes for pretty ladies," he offered, maybe stretching the truth a little.

The Librarian nodded sagely and lifted the counter between them, turning to head deeper into a part of the library where the common riffraff like him was usually excluded. Hopefully, she just wanted to show him a book and wasn't aiming for some special privacy.

Down a short hall, around a corner, to a door that she opened with a key. Inside, more books on stacks, but the room smelled old. Musty. Tired.

She moved to a certain stack and picked up a pair of white gloves, putting them on and handing him another pair. She pulled a book from a shelf and placed it nearby, on a desk in the corner, nodding to him.

"Only touch it with gloves," she said sternly. "Nothing leaves this room. I'll come back for you in an hour or so."

Gunderson nodded and let her slip by, breathing a sigh of relief.

He put the gloves on and sat. This tome was leather-bound, but not a leather he was familiar with. A little voice in the back of his mind whispered human flesh, but he ignored it and carefully opened it to read about Abdul Alhazred, the so-called Mad Arab, and his literary creation, Al Azif.

The front half of the book was a brief history of necromancy and other dark arts, written in that weirdly idyllic moment before the First War when Edward was king.

The back was more of an encyclopedia, listing references to a bunch of people he'd never heard of, as well as things like The Book of Eibon, the Celaeno Fragments, and the Cthäat Aquadingen.

This latter one drew his attention, as it referenced The Old Ones that Madame al-Taghut had mentioned not wanting to summon. Reading about them, he could see why. Old Ones. Elder Gods. Wars outside of time.

Peachy.

Then Gunderson reached an entry that made his blood run cold in his veins. An immortal priestess of the Old Ones, described with a very particular tattoo in a very special place. The scholar's account listed her impossible, ageless beauty, a gift from some being for serving them.

A simple pencil sketch accompanied the chronicle, done in just a few strokes, but Gunderson recognized her. She looked twenty in the picture, but he knew that was a lie. In 1955, she still looked forty-ish, some fifty years after the book had been published, drawing on older materials.

Had losing the book in 1924 caused her to lose the favor of the Old Ones? Was she actually aging now, however much slower than a normal human?

What was she?

No, he knew that answer. A woman, given the option to be young and beautiful forever, in a world where men rarely valued them for their brains? Almost every woman he'd ever known would have probably leapt at the chance.

She hadn't been lying about summoning the Old Ones back to destroy the world. Of at least that much Gunderson was certain. What would happen if he returned the book to her?

What would van Gelder do? Gunderson was certain he'd seen the correct book in the library, however false the reasons that got him into the room.

He would need answers. And there was only one place he could get them.

———

GUNDERSON SAID hello to the same maid as before. Got seated in that same doctor's office of a front room while he waited. Left his hat on the couch beside him again as something of a concrete highway barrier.

She was wearing more clothes this time. For what it was worth. Long, flowing dress that reminded him of robes from a movie rather than something everyday people wore, gathered at the waist to show off her figure. White, but linen this time, and thick enough to cover everything thankfully. Hung to her shins and didn't cover the arms, so he got to see some level of dark, tanned flesh. Just not the interesting bits.

Gunderson was okay with that.

Madame al-Taghut had her hair pulled back into a simple tail in a way that made her look almost like a hawk, which was another interesting motif, considering her apparent history and possible age. A few gray roots were more obvious this way.

She entered with far less flamboyance today. Not prim and proper, but also not competing with a Tijuana prostitute. Gunderson was seated in the same place as three days ago, so she did the same.

They studied each other. He could see the pencil sketch image someone had done in the Nineteenth Century. He wondered what she saw.

"And how are you today, detective?" she asked.

"Concerned," he answered after a long beat.

No good was going to come of lying to the woman. She had hired him to do a thing, and he was going to.

She smiled, like she could read his soul.

"You've seen the book," she said triumphantly.

"I have," Gunderson agreed. "Sitting out in the open, as though it was nothing. I presume that much is camouflage."

"And your concerns, Mr. Gunderson?" she tilted her head just a little to study him.

"What year were you born, Madame al-Taghut?" he asked simply.

She started to reply and stopped herself.

"You know," she accused.

"I suspect," he countered. "Won't change anything. Just idle curiosity more than anything. I'm hoping that your possession of the book means that the Old Ones will remain bound by the sigils of the Elder Gods for now, and that nothing terrible is likely to happen."

"What would you do?" she asked, leaning forward a little now and eyeing him closer. "You've obviously done your homework since last I saw you. Where did you look?"

"In my line of work, a man's got to have all manner of friends and acquaintances," Gunderson said. "Found a drawing in a book that looked like a close relative of yours."

"Ah, Herr Matthau," she smiled now, warm and inviting. "I knew it was probably a mistake talking to the man, but I never expected it to matter all that much. What did you think?"

"I think you are that old, and probably that dangerous," he answered honestly. "But I'm hoping that this is a lesser evil kind of situation, because van Gelder is a great enough evil by himself."

"You are correct, Gunderson," she said. "Not many people understand that, but I have no interest in reviving a group of homicidal beings that will bring about the end of days and unleash their chaos upon the universe."

"Guardian of the way?" he asked.

"Yog-Sothoth is the Way, and the Key," she intoned,

sounding more like a chant than an answer. "While he remains bound, dread Cthulhu cannot rise from his eternal, watery grave."

"Lovely," Gunderson replied. "Anything I need to worry about, if I return for an overdue library book?"

Again, that tongue just wetting the bottom lip. The little bite that suggested she was even more aroused than that librarian had been. Gunderson didn't sleep with his clients.

Or even ex-clients, once he had solved their problem. Too much risk of solving some future case in such a way that a beautiful dame fell into your bed.

Femme fatale, in every sense of the word.

"Wait here," she instructed him, standing in a swish of linen and exiting deeper into the building.

Gunderson leaned back and thought happier thoughts. Nothing in the back of the house he ever wanted to see or know. That much was certain.

Madame al-Taghut returned in just a few minutes, but felt like she had been gone half an eternity.

"Stand up," she ordered him, so he did, towering over the much smaller woman. "Hold out your left arm."

Gunderson shrugged and did.

She pushed back the sleeve of his jacket and then unbuttoned the cuff of his shirt, revealing his old watch, which was in need of repairs sometime soon. Maybe next week, if he survived and had a few spare bucks lying around after this.

Before he could react, Madame al-Taghut slapped a silver bracelet around his wrist and muttered something he didn't catch. The thing clamped tight with an audible snap, all by itself as she stepped back.

"What the hell?" he asked, reaching for it, but it would not budge.

Gunderson studied it, looking for a seam he might wedge

a chisel into, but the silver band seemed to be a single thing, like it had been forged around his wrist. Maybe an inch wide. Silver. Hammered finish rather than a shine.

"This will protect you from various creatures," she smiled up at him. "If van Gelder is a warlock, he might have a creature of the deep protecting him."

Gunderson wondered if that butler was more than human. Or less.

"You'll take it off when I bring you the book?" he snarled at her, unable to find a way to sound casual about it.

"Indeed, Gunderson," she nodded, smiling seductively. "You will be richly rewarded for returning both to me."

He suspected that the money on the table was only part of what might be available, if Gunderson wanted to push his luck. And experience nightmares with tentacles.

"Good enough," he said, reaching for his hat and cramming it down on his head more as a statement of purpose than anything sartorial. "See you soon."

She was still smiling as he stomped out the front door and down the sidewalk. The alternative to stomping would have been to grab the woman and kiss her. She'd certainly been inviting it, along with a lot of other things, if he'd been reading her right.

Tentacles, wrapped around him and holding him in place like heels.

Gunderson threw himself into the Mallory and got it to start, wondering if he'd still need a cold shower by the time he got back to his apartment.

NIGHT.

Gunderson had a few other concurrent cases going, so he'd spent a few days on those, just killing time right now and letting his target get a little lulled back to sleep from being poked and prodded by a tall Swede. Madame al-Taghut had said that there were no impending occlusions or stellar alignments that would make it easier to open the way. At least not for a while.

Whatever that meant.

Good. The last thing Gunderson needed was to try to do all this in the middle of a ticking bomb scenario.

The same house, on that same fake hill so it could look down on neighbors. Trees that hadn't been cut down when everything was built meant that there were a lot of shadows to work with.

Gunderson had parked the Mallory several blocks away and walked in. There was a risk of dogs and nosy neighbors, but he had learned a long time ago how to slink with the best of them. It had him on the same side of the street, down a few houses now and watching.

The street lights weren't that close together around here. Porch lights didn't do much to illuminate front yards that tended to be bounded by hedges or low brick walls that were decorative rather than defensive. But it made it easier for him to slip in and out of the darker patches.

Once, his left wrist pulsed with a cold so sharp he wondered if his hand would go numb, but the pain passed just as fast as it came. Detection spell thwarted? Defensive spell deflected? Monster trying to sniff his passage?

Gunderson knew that there was more to the world than met the eye. Most PIs never saw things beyond the mundane, but he'd been out there a few times. Maybe a few too many. He paused now to smell the spring jasmine just blooming.

It didn't feel like his last night on Earth, but they never did, and he'd come through too much of a World War and a Homecoming to take it for granted.

He stopped under a willow whose branches hung down

like bloody whips and turned completely in place, just letting his ears mark any sound around him. Nothing stood out. He wondered if that bracelet hid him from prying eyes.

Gunderson didn't figure he'd have gotten a straight answer out of her, so he hadn't asked. Simple as that.

Still, nothing.

The house sat on a couple of acres wide and a couple more deep. Old money neighborhood where you weren't packed cheek in jowl with others. Not like Gunderson's flat down in the basin.

But no fences either, front or back. He'd made sure of that when he'd come the first time. And a few other times earlier on other cases, before it had been necessary to actually do something this monumentally stupid.

No fences meant no dogs. Again, he'd taken the time on the previous visit to be sure, but with a constantly-changing variety of still-innocent waifs around that made sense. Too hard to train dogs who the dangerous people might be. That left the butler, most likely.

He moved to his left. The neighboring house on that side was essentially dark, but for a third story bedroom window behind shades. The no-man's-land between them was bushes rather than a fence. Mostly a dogwood hedge that someone had planted to demarcate things, and both sides kept more or less under control. Still, it let him reach the first one and squat down, like an extension of the greenery.

Patience was the key here. No mystical alignments tonight meant that he was on the schedule of van Gelder's libido and the butler's endurance. Both would run out at some point, especially as there wasn't a party going on.

At least out in the open. Closed doors, and all that.

Gunderson waited nearly five minutes, letting the insects mask most sound and adjusting his eyes to the darker confines of the side yard, away from street lights.

Nothing. The silver bracelet didn't feel heavy or cold right now, so he hoped that was a good enough sign. He rose and slid along the hedge like a moving bush rather than a man.

The nearly-new Smith and Wesson Model 29 under his arm was a comforting weight. It was always loaded with silver bullets because of another case a few years ago, but they would hit just as hard as lead if something didn't have those sorts of allergies.

Right now, he was hoping he didn't have to use it. Quiet neighborhood that would call the cops for a gunshot. LAPD would be here in a jiffy, given the folks and the money that lived around here.

He studied the side of van Gelder's house, but the windows on this side were dark. Library was on the back corner, where the windows were about eight feet up from the way the house rose.

He'd known a few cat burglars and ninjas in his time, but Gunderson had never learned those sorts of skills, so he would need to enter from a door. Given the Napoleonic complex for a porch out front, he assumed the back would be a better bet anyway. Shorter trip inside from what he remembered. Less risk of running into anyone.

Gunderson made it to the corner of the building and peeked carefully around, hoping that none of the girls had felt the need to skinny dip naked tonight. Silence. Close enough to dark, with only a few lights framing corners and marking the pool itself so nobody accidentally fell in.

He paused and breathed. From here, he could hear music playing. Sounded like a phonograph, but Gunderson didn't recognize the symphony. At least it wasn't a jitterbug or a ragtime playing. Small favors.

Gunderson leaned out enough to look up and saw a light on a window overhead. The window was open, as well, spilling a violin sonata, quietly backed by the whole woodwind section.

Good. If van Gelder was listening to music, maybe he'd stay upstairs. Hopefully, whatever girl was with him could keep his attention focused, too.

Nothing sounded except his breathing.

Gunderson slid across the back of the house and up three stone steps like a night ghost, listening with his ears but also paying attention to that thing al-Taghut had given him.

Nothing at all.

He finally approached the mostly-glass back door and looked inside. The moon was about to set, so things were as dark as they ever got in LA at night. That, plus a few nightlights inside marking the small dining area to one side and the oversized kitchen to the other. Far more than a bachelor like van Gelder needed, but possibly not enough for some of the larger parties he was known to host.

Not that Gunderson had ever been invited. Or would have attended.

Rule number one: never assume your opponent is a genius or a fool. Most people fall in the middle of a parabolic curve.

Gunderson put a gloved hand on the doorknob and turned it slightly, just to confirm that someone had remembered to lock it before retiring for the evening. More than once, he'd slipped in someplace without resorting to the picks, but he needed them now.

Out of a pocket, he pulled two shaped pieces of steel and knelt down to slide them home. In the back of his mind, he wondered if tentacles were about to reach out and grab him. A few quick flicks and it was done.

But wasn't that always the case when you approached something delicate and sensitive with care and professionalism?

He rose and put the picks away in a jacket pocket for now, turning the knob silently before pushing it inwards. Right about now was when the prosecutable crimes would start stacking up, if he got caught.

Of course, if van Gelder was what Madame al-Taghut proclaimed, he might not even call the police.

Gunderson slid in and closed the door silently without bothering to lock it. Most people encountering something like that would presume they had forgotten and just fix it.

He stepped off to one side and stood perfectly still in a shadow cast by a corner and the refrigerator, straining to smell anything out of the ordinary. Dinner had included both onions and garlic, so presumably van Gelder wasn't also a vampire.

He waited for nearly thirty seconds before he moved. The house faintly echoed with the music upstairs still, so hopefully no one would need to come down. If they decided to go for a midnight swim, he could always go out the front door.

The architecture in here was mundane, for all the exoticness of the furnishings. Hallway right down the middle, dividing the ground floor into two wings. Gunderson slipped out of the kitchen into that hall and stayed along the wall to his right, checking that none of the pictures seemed to be alive and watching him walk by.

He'd only seen that once, but once was too many.

To the library door, still ajar with darkness beyond. He listened. Music and crickets, nothing else.

Gunderson slipped into the library now. More crimes, because van Gelder would presume why he was here. Probably correctly, unless the man had an entire arcane library tucked in among the various mundane tomes and folios.

The thing on his wrist reacted to something in the room,

growing cool but not that sharp, arctic blast he'd felt earlier. Gunderson waved it around and it seemed to point him at the book, still on the lectern. Other places reacted as well, but not as much. Just kisses on the inside of his wrist, like an amorous Egyptian woman playing.

Gunderson growled inside his head and got back to work. Enough light came in the windows that he didn't need the pencil flashlight he had brought with him on this raid. He walked up to the book and felt his wrist grow heavy and cold.

A sound at the door caused him to spin in place, his right hand diving into his jacket for the Smith.

Overhead lights came on, nearly blinding him.

Gunderson blinked hard.

There was a thing, a creature standing there, starting across the room at him. van Gelder stood behind it, half hidden in shadows and darkness.

The beast had one, great eye in the middle of a face where the nose and mouth had been slipped to the bottom. Green, scaly skin and a fin like a trout's mohawk running from forehead to neck. Arms like an ape, reaching past his knees, ending in terrible, rending claws that were even now reaching for him. It walked on stubby legs, like a woman in reverse, all torso and no leg.

Gunderson cleared his revolver, but the thing was on him before he could shoot.

Then Gunderson's soul turned to ice.

His left wrist rose of its own volition and intercepted the claw coming at his face, like a fellow downtown who taught Chinese fighting arts. The cold was so intense he wondered if he would lose that hand from frostbite.

But the claw grasped his arm, closed on it.

The creature screamed in agony. Let go and jumped back,

stumbling over an ottoman and falling into a display case with a crash of glass.

"What have you done?" van Gelder screamed in surprised rage as he stepped into the room.

Gunderson would have answered, but anything he said right now would have been a lie. He had no clue, other than Madame al-Taghut had apparently just saved his ass.

Crucifixes and vampires.

Gunderson shook his head to clear cobwebs that had taken root in all corners. van Gelder raised his hands like a stage magician and began chanting something in a language that seemed all vowels.

Made the hackles on the back of Gunderson's neck stand up like electricity.

Before he could move, a flash of lightning erupted out of van Gelder's hands, aimed at Gunderson's heart. Except that it stopped just short of frying Gunderson's soul.

van Gelder stood there in shock, jaw dropped open almost as far as Gunderson's.

"Kill him!" van Gelder yelled at his lizard attack dog thing.

The beast reached out and grabbed Gunderson's leg.

Gunderson wasn't having any of that. He knelt and touched his wrist on the thing's gigantic eye, as large as a tea saucer. White light flashed with an ugly sizzle and Gunderson found himself on his ass, halfway across the room. A chair had stopped him from slamming into a glass-fronted book case.

van Gelder hadn't been so lucky. Gunderson could see blood dripping from the man's back as they both started to staggered to their feet.

"What have you done, you bastard?!?" the sorcerer screamed in a fury.

Gunderson didn't bother asking, unsure if he'd done it or

Madame al-Taghut. Beast was dead, eye and head burned out. That was good enough.

Man over there started chanting again. Gunderson decided that it was time to raise the stakes.

He fired.

Silver or not, it hit hard and punched through, pushing van Gelder backwards against those books again with a look of utter shock on his face. Like nobody had ever shot him before.

Gunderson could have told him how much something like that hurt.

First one had taken the man where his heart would be but only staggered him. Gunderson put the next one into his face, since the man was still making noises.

Normally, Gunderson didn't believe in violence. Certainly wasn't the shoot-first type. At the same time, he didn't figure he was actually in the wrong. That thing had brought a Deep One, from the sketch Gunderson had seen in the book. And cast lightning at him.

Both made this self-defense.

Second bullet broke something in the man. Gunderson wondered if he even had a heart to stop, or if the bullet had just opened a new hole in his lungs and slowed van Gelder down a little bit.

Nothing like silver spiking the brain when you have to be certain.

Gunderson walked closer, lungs rasping like a bellows. van Gelder wasn't moving, but Gunderson still had that monstrous .44 pointed at him, just in case. The Deep One was a half-cooked fish that wasn't bothering anyone ever again.

He reached down with his left wrist and touched the sorcerer. Faintest spark, but nothing like he'd had before. And even that faded.

Gunderson stood up again and blew out a heavy breath. No way to explain any of this to the cops. Even if they would believe him.

Gunfire would wake someone. Two shots would sound like an assassination. Police would be called. He didn't have long.

Gunderson looked around the room and spied an old-style kerosene lamp on a shelf. Glass with a wick, chased in either brass or rose gold. Didn't matter. Would serve his purpose.

He retrieved it and poured a bunch on the bookcase van Gelder had died against, as well as over the man himself. Old books. Old wood.

Hopefully, the heat would melt the silver bullets enough to deform them and nobody would ever be able to compare lines and grooves.

He moved to the book and took it under one arm. Big. Heavy. Awkward.

Worth at least one man's life tonight.

A sound at the door nearly got the girl killed as Gunderson spun around and pointed his cannon at her.

She gasped and leapt back. Gunderson was on her before she could move.

"How many girls are in the house?" he demanded.

He didn't have a hand free to grab the girl, so Gunderson had to rely on force of will to hold her in place. Her pupils were a little off, as well, so he presumed van Gelder had given her something to overcome any lingering inhibitions.

Good thing Gunderson wasn't a necromancer. Might have to raise that stinking bastard from the dead again, just to kill him a second time.

"What…?" the redhead asked.

"The building is on fire," Gunderson yelled in her face now. "You need to get the girls out. How many?"

"Me and Kimmie and Joan," she whimpered.

Gunderson heard more noise from the foyer, coming down the stairs.

"What's going on?" a woman's voice asked. Girl's voice. Barely legal in this state.

Gunderson propelled the redhead towards the front, where two other shadows were visible against the glass on either side of the door.

"All three of you need to get out!" Gunderson let his fear sound like rage calling down the wrath of Heaven. "The building is on fire. Out the front door right now before you get hurt!"

The redhead staggered ahead of him. The blond seemed sober enough. She opened the double doors and stepped onto the porch, wearing a thin negligee that hardly covered more than Madame al-Taghut had, that first time.

All three ended up out there, so Gunderson pushed the door closed and locked it. That should keep them safe until the police and fire department arrived.

He raced back to the library and studied the room. The bracelet reacted to several other places, but he didn't have time. Truth be told, Gunderson didn't care, either. He found a box of matches that had been with the lamp and tossed a lit one onto the kerosene-soaked corpse of a pimp and white slaver, watching long enough confirm that it caught, racing up onto the bookshelf and igniting whatever power and wisdom the man had accumulated in life.

Gunderson went out the back door and into the night as sirens approached.

GUNDERSON SAT in the doctor's office front room with a paper-wrapped satchel under his hat. The maid had withdrawn, leaving him alone with his thoughts. Probably a smart move on her part, if she was the slightest bit empathic.

Madame al-Taghut arrived. Dressed Western-style for once. Long skirt. Buttoned up shirt. Long blazer almost a tunic in length. She wore makeup like an American housewife and smiled at him as she took her spot on the other couch.

Demure.

He wasn't the least bit fooled.

"Traveling?" Gunderson asked anyway.

"Indeed," she smiled warmly. "Once van Gelder was removed from the equation, I knew that my time here would be short."

"Because I would be bringing you the book as soon as I had time for a shower and change of clothes, plus stopping for breakfast," Gunderson stated rather than asked.

"You are a man of your word, Gunderson," she said, eyes somehow turning both serious and mischievous at the same time. "Everyone I have consulted agrees on that point. So I only needed to pack up the few things I had brought with me and prepare to depart."

He grunted. Gestured vaguely.

"Would you like to unwrap it?" he asked.

"I can feel its presence and power from here," she answered. "Thank you."

"You hired me to do a thing," he said in turn.

"Give me your hand and I will remove the token," she gestured.

Gunderson placed his hand on hers and let her push everything out of the way to expose that silver bracelet that felt like it weighed as much as his car this morning. But it was a metaphorical weight.

On his soul, rather than his arm.

She muttered something and it popped open with a flash

of silver light that he might have missed had he blinked. Madame al-Taghut slipped it into her jacket pocket and studied him now.

"And now time for your reward," she said.

Gunderson couldn't help the flinch of tenseness that ran through his body, but he didn't do more than that.

"Oh, not like that, Gunderson," she chuckled throatily. "You asked for money and nothing more."

He nodded and she pulled an envelope from the inner breast pocket of her jacket, handing it to him.

"I included a bonus, for your honesty and for helping me deal with that fool van Gelder," she said.

Gunderson tucked it into his pocket unopened. He'd deal with it later, after he was away from this place and all the emotions she stirred up in a soul he'd thought too jaded to react to a beautiful woman again.

She smiled, like she could read his mind. Or maybe his soul. Gunderson's mother had always said that most men weren't much more deep or complicated than a mud puddle.

But this woman made him dream of tentacled monsters emerging from the darkest depths.

"Happy to be of service," he said, mostly angry at himself for reasons he didn't feel like exploring.

Gunderson grabbed his hat and rose. He turned and made it to the door before she could stand, mostly so he would be away from the woman, in case she decided to be vulnerable at him.

"Would it be so bad?" she asked as he opened the portal back to the sad, dry, mundane world.

"No," Gunderson replied.

He fled.

GUNDERSON WAS SEATED at the counter of his favorite diner. The one not that many blocks from the office he was required by law to keep. The summer heat was stifling as June grudgingly gave way to the hotter months. He had his tie loose and wore his lightest weight brown suit, drinking an iced coffee rather than soda pop or anything hot.

He'd finished a burger and was chasing down the last few french fries left on his plate before he went back to see what trouble the world had thrown up on his shore while he was out. His secretary Annabelle could handle anything and anybody for an hour or two. If they got frisky she'd probably stab them with her knitting needles.

Some unknown sixth sense warned him. Gunderson looked up and turned completely to his right to watch her enter the diner. He wasn't the only one.

Young.

Twenty-two, maybe. Raven black hair, long and thick, pulled back into a braid. Breasts like torpedoes about to sink a Jap tin can. Body like a goddess come down to bless your entire day just for being in it for five seconds.

She wore a knee-length dress in cornflower blue, with a black belt that seemed to make her ageless, innocent, and deadly, all at once. This vision turned and smiled at him.

Gunderson would have liked to have said he'd met her mother, but he'd be lying. She looked more like that sketch now than she had, but she'd lost the book in '24, so she had perhaps aged without it. Not thirty-plus years, but some.

Madame al-Taghut walked right up to him and took the empty stool on his right.

Gunderson nodded his head. He would have tipped his hat but it was sitting on the counter, where the waitress had arrived to take charge. Or take orders.

Madame al-Taghut pointed at Gunderson's iced coffee.

"I'll have one of those, please," she said in a young,

innocent voice. Alto. Throaty with promises of passion and power if you reached up and ran your fingers through her hair, maybe pausing halfway and taking a really hard hold and tugging it.

Gunderson remembered to breathe. The waitress left them alone.

The Goddess smiled a secret smile up at him.

"You remind me of someone I knew once," he finally offered in a careful, distant voice.

"Was she very beautiful?" this woman-child asked, all bright and innocent and lethal and cold and warm.

"More than the moon," Gunderson replied. "But just as deadly as she was beautiful."

"Did you ever see her again?" she asked, playing along with this game as if they were well-met strangers sitting in a diner somewhere having lunch companionably.

"I did not," Gunderson said. "She hired me for a thing and I did it. Got her back some stolen property that was of tremendous personal importance, and we both went on our ways."

"That sounds sad," she observed, her accent just starting to appear around the edges now. "Are men like you never allowed happy endings to your stories?"

Gunderson grabbed a few fries and stuffed them in his mouth as an excuse to not answer immediately.

"Men like you are hard because the world demands it," she continued, knowingly. "But compassionate enough to rescue three kittens from a fire for no reason that would have mattered to anyone else. All that passion has to remain bottled up, all the time, doesn't it?"

Gunderson grunted. Safer that way. She didn't need to hear about the nights where the whiskey was what got him to sleep. Or the cold showers and nightmares about tentacles reaching out to pull him down into the depths forever.

"It's not that bad," she said ambivalently. "The initial costs can be high, but over the longer term the price is tiny for the rewards."

He studied her body now, like it was the reward she might be offering. She had then, as well. Hard and young. Proud with that first blush of youth, right when it poised on the edge of adulthood. Coupled with a mind that was at least two centuries old, if that German scholar had gotten it right.

Gunderson suspected that she'd lied to the man then.

"How far back do you remember?" he asked in a quiet voice.

The waitress returned with another glass of iced coffee for the girl and a refill for him, interrupting everything except that wicked gleam in the girl's eyes.

"You wouldn't believe me," she murmured with a seductive grin.

"Three months ago, I might not have," Gunderson countered. "We were both other people then."

He was three months older. She was twenty-five years younger.

He still dreamed about that tattoo, wondering if it had scarred her flesh enough that he might feel it, were they pressed against each other. Dancing, or something.

"The Elder Gods demand great sacrifices among those that they have tasked with keeping the Old Ones trapped," she said in a voice as normal as talking about baseball. "But they understand that it can be difficult, finding allies among our kind, so they make up for it, for those willing to walk that path."

"That path," Gunderson echoed.

"And you intend to walk a different one, don't you?" Madame/Girl al-Taghut asked in a voice far more grown up than her face.

Almost as old as her eyes.

Gunderson caught himself short of making a rude comment. Or a sarcastic, self-deprecating one. Or even just leaning over and kissing her.

They needed honesty, the two of them. Thus it has always been, even as short as their love affair had lasted.

Love affair?

Yes, he could call it that. Gunderson still woke in a hot or cold sweat with her name on his lips. Still found his hands out-stretched, aching to touch her. To grip her. To pull her close and taste the texture of her skin.

"What do you fear?" she asked, taking a drink.

"Everything," he replied. "And nothing."

"Yes, I see that about you," she smiled sadly. "You fear me, almost as much as you fear for me. I can take care of myself, Gunderson."

"Indeed," he agreed. "And probably me and the rest as well. I suppose I fear the cost?"

"Living forever is a cost?" she asked, a bit surprised.

"We did things," Gunderson said, eyes unfocused as he fell into his memory. "Saw things. Stopped a brutally evil man from conquering the world, but the costs were not born equally, and many of us came home broken."

"It has been a decade," she noted. "Have you healed any?"

"Some," he shrugged. "I can't be a police detective anymore. Tried being a cook, but that wasn't it. Did a number of other things. Even just wandered. Eventually, I ended up here and found a niche that allowed me to use my gifts and my skills positively."

"You resist evil," she said.

"And chaos," Gunderson agreed. "But it will never be enough. I cannot defeat them. But I must try."

"It will not allow you happiness?" she pressed, turned towards him and leaned in just enough to invite a kiss.

He considered it. Resisted that siren call as well, knowing that rocks lurked under the water nearby if he did.

"I don't know what happiness looks like," he finally admitted.

Gunderson leaned in close enough to touch cheeks, but couldn't bring himself to kiss her. To taste her. It would be a delicacy, a maelstrom that would pull him under and keep him there until he drowned, tentacles hovering nearby if he tried to escape later.

She pulled back finally, breaking that warm touch enough to look him in the eyes.

"You have time," she said. "If you keep yourself alive, all things become possible if you change your mind later."

"That is what frightens me," Gunderson said.

He set the glass down and grabbed his hat as he rose. Tossed a couple of bucks on the counter to cover everything and a tip. Jammed his hat down onto his over-thick skull and nodded to this goddess who had descended from the heavens to bless him a second time.

He didn't look back as he walked out the door.

BLACKMAILERS

THE GUNDERSON CASE FILES (004)
BLACKMAILERS

GUNDERSON WAS ACTUALLY in his office for once when a client wandered in, wonder of wonders. Usually, he was off doing things and his secretary Annabelle, the watchdog of his domain, would either find him or leave a note. But she'd needed to run some errands this afternoon, so he was watching the storefront himself instead.

Probably just as well. The man who entered was a cop Gunderson knew, although he was wearing a sedate, brown suit instead of his police uniform. Just opened the outer door, looked through the open inner door to Gunderson's office and strode right in like he owned the place. Cops were like that in this town.

The afternoon was late. Gunderson thought about it, then pulled a bottle and a pair of glasses from the bottom drawer as Captain Flanagan silently entered and sat in one of the chairs with a heavy sigh. He poured a glass and slipped it across to the man.

"Whatever it is, I don't suppose it's going to be good, is it, Captain Flanagan?" Gunderson asked.

The man nodded and took a sip, so Gunderson did as well.

Captain Tobias Flanagan. LAPD. A political cop, rather than a field man like Gunderson had been, back when he'd been a cop. Tall and lean, though neither as much as Gunderson. Just about fifty, if Gunderson remembered correctly. Sandy blond hair three-quarters faded now.

One of the few honest cops Gunderson knew on the force. LA Sheriff's Department was even worse these day.

"I, we, need to hire you, Gunderson," the man said in a tired voice.

Sounded like someone had been up all night alternately praying and cursing. Lines on his face and bags under his eyes didn't help.

"Department can't help?" Gunderson asked, but it was mostly *pro forma*.

The man had walked into his office late in the afternoon on a Tuesday, sat down, and was now sipping his rye.

"Not without causing more problems than they'll solve," the Captain looked up now. "Too many old skeletons will get pulled out of the closet and the press will have a field day with us all. Need to keep this quiet. Joyce suggested that you might be the right man to run it all down and help sort it out."

Gunderson liked Joyce. She was a friend, an old Hollywood starlet from the early days who had never quite made it past chorus girl. She'd ended up marrying shady money instead, and then inheriting it all when some of her first husband's gangster friends killed him over a shipment of illicit hooch.

Her second husband was a banker. About as quiet and thoughtful a man as Gunderson had ever met. But Joyce still had all sorts of interesting contacts from the old days, and occasionally seemed intent on keeping Gunderson in business all by herself, just by referring friends with issues.

When Gunderson hesitated, Flanagan spoke up again.

"Money to pay you is coming out of a slush fund budget we keep around for informers and off the books things," the man continued. "But the cause is righteous."

Gunderson nodded and sipped at his own glass. Dirty money was dirty money, but Flanagan was generally a good man in a corrupt city. They weren't pals, but Gunderson knew the man well enough to appreciate that Flanagan would smile at using dirty money to do good deeds.

"So what's the case?" Gunderson asked with a twisted smile.

GUNDERSON GRUNTED to himself as he counted houses and looked at numbers on the fronts, driving almost at an idle down a shaded street. Newport Beach was something of a bedroom community, but had been growing by leaps and bounds since the war ended. Orange County was still mostly farms and ranches, but Gunderson could see that changing over the next thirty years, as people spilled out of Los Angeles and went south along the coast. Inland was too damned hot, once you got over the mountains up towards San Bernardino or Riverside. They wouldn't go there until later.

Still, he found the house he was looking for and pulled to the curb just a little past it, slipping the old '49 Mallory into the morning shade of an orange tree and killing the engine. He took a moment to think about everything Flanagan had told him last night before getting out and putting his hat on. Sea breeze carried salt and oranges today, and it was cool enough that he wasn't sweating in his brown suit.

Gunderson made his way to the front door of a little bungalow on a postage stamp of dirt with a strip of grass small enough you could mow it with scissors. There was an old fig tree in the side yard thinking about taking everything over soon. He knocked at the screen and waited, looking in through the open door behind it.

A shadow appeared quickly enough and approached. Small man, but part of that was a hunch from age. Gunderson guessed him to be in his mid-sixties. Pear-shaped and mostly bald, but the brown eyes held a twinkle of intelligence as he looked up.

"Name's Gunderson," he said. "Flanagan sent me."

Rather than speak, the man pushed the screen open enough to make a statement and then slipped back into the room. Gunderson caught the door and followed.

The interior of the front room wasn't dark, but there were no lights on in here. That left it just dim enough for someone out in the sun trying to see inside would only see shadows.

Gunderson sat in a chair and watched the man back through the doorway into the kitchen as he fussily started a tea pot without asking. But that was fine. Gunderson would have tea if that was what was needed to get the rest of the story.

Soon enough, the pot was on to boil and they were facing each other across a coffee table strewn with picture books. The wall to one side held hard-cover tomes. A few of the titles even suggested that the man had once been a cop.

Lt. Derwin had been a Narcotics Detective back in '36, nearly twenty years ago. Back when Gunderson had still been walking a beat up in Seattle.

"Tobias is an old friend," Derwin said. "When he was just a rookie detective, he was my partner. Back in those days, we were just moving on from dealing with bootleggers to harder drugs, but it was still stuff coming up from Mexico or across from the Orient."

Gunderson nodded. Tobias Flanagan had told him some of those old stories, back when crazy people put on colorful costumes and ran around with silly code names and catch phrases. But the Thirties had been weird. All that had kind of faded out in most places by about 1940, only to suffer a shot of ardent rejuvenation after Pearl Harbor.

Gunderson had joined the army. Others had dug out their silly costumes and gone after Nazi infiltrators and criminals who hadn't gotten the patriotism memo.

It was only after the war when that sort of thing had mostly faded again. Even the comic books had completely changed these days.

"Tobias told you everything?" Derwin asked.

"He did, but I'd like to hear it in your words, Lieutenant," Gunderson replied.

"Charles," the man corrected him. "I haven't been Lt. Derwin in…a long time. I'm just a retired duffer these days, living on my pension and alone."

"But a letter came in the mail, Charles?" Gunderson prompted him. "Blackmail?"

"Yes, Mr. Gunderson," Derwin nodded. "Threatening to disclose some dark and terrible secrets that should be left in the past."

"Without getting too deeply into those secrets, I would like to know who might have known enough to blackmail you," Gunderson said.

Sure enough, the man flinched some. Wanted to clam right up, but whatever it was had been bad enough that a retired police detective lieutenant had reached out to his former partner, who had gone a little rogue himself to hire a straight PI using crooked money.

"Did you live in LA before the war, Gunderson?" Charles asked. "Tobias said you had been a cop, but I didn't recognize your name."

"I was up in Seattle," Gunderson said. "Walked a beat from '34 to '40 and then made detective. Did that until I enlisted in '42. Got out in '46 and returned to civilian life but couldn't be a cop anymore. Ended up down here by '51."

"Couldn't be a cop anymore, Gunderson?" Charles asked.

"My heart wasn't in it," he replied with a sigh. "Tried other things in other places. P.I. lets me put my size and skills to work, but I can't see myself ever wearing a badge again."

"A lot of men only partly returned from the war," Derwin nodded sagely. "I have seen it myself. The terrible traumas they survived. So maybe you'll understand."

Gunderson sat back and waited. In the kitchen, the pot began to whistle, interrupting everything, so Derwin rose and went off to the kitchen.

"Coffee or tea?" the man finally asked as he exited the room, apparently distracted before.

"Coffee's fine."

Trauma. Interesting choice of words. Captain Flanagan hadn't known what had happened. Only that a blackmailer thought he could get money out of Derwin, and Derwin hadn't denied it to his old partner.

They had asked an outsider who could be trusted to keep his mouth shut to get involved, instead.

A tired Charles Derwin returned a few minutes later and put a mug in front of him, so Gunderson sipped at it.

"Something happened in 1936, Gunderson," Derwin began, both hands wrapped around the mug like he was drawing heat from it, even though the day was perfect in the low seventies outside. A shiver passed through Derwin's frame nonetheless.

But everyone has fears and coping mechanisms. Gunderson could see this one being the thing that kept Derwin from diving headfirst into a bottle until he drowned.

Maybe it would have been better if he had?

Gunderson nodded to keep the man talking, checking the story about the fragments Flanagan had shared.

"There were still heroes in those days, Gunderson. Stepped right off a comic book page like Flash Gordon or Buck Rogers come to life," Derwin said. "L.A. had her fair share, although places like Boston and New York were bigger in those days and had more. Are you familiar with a particular one named Miss Lynx?"

Gunderson hadn't been. And hadn't taken a half-day to swing by a library and bribe a librarian to find him the right records. He'd do that after he left here, most likely.

He shook his head.

"She was a costumed crimefighter, Gunderson," Derwin said, his voice bleeding over into pain and regret now. An old man whose ghosts weren't going to be satisfied to only haunt his dreams. "Unlike many of them, she didn't have any special powers beyond a stubborn belief that the job was necessary to do. Started when she was eighteen, although none of us knew it at the time. That was 1932 and bootleggers and smugglers were getting out of hand. I imagine it was just as bad out of Canada?"

Gunderson nodded. Before his time, though, since Prohibition had ended for good in December of 1933.

"A goodly number of bad guys took to wearing costumes as well in those days, mostly to hide their identities, but also to frighten people when costumed heroes started taking inspiration from the Scarlet Pimpernel or Douglas Fairbanks," Derwin continued. "Scholars with a dabbling of arcane lore got into it, as did inventors and acrobats. Miss

Lynx wasn't the best known, or most successful, but she had an excellent record foiling organized crime around here, seemingly with inside knowledge that nobody could understand."

"Because she got it from you," Gunderson prompted when the man fell silent.

Derwin looked up from his coffee with pained eyes.

"I had no idea she was my own daughter, detective," he whispered. "I was a widower even then, raising Emily and Gerald with a maid, but being a cop meant I was out a lot. Long enough for her to decide to do something about crime in this city even though she was just a teenager. Apparently she would sneak into my office at home and pick the lock on my file cabinet to read things."

Gunderson nodded. He'd gotten a similar story from Flanagan last night.

"What happened in '36?" Gunderson asked, watching the man's body language.

That was the piece Flanagan hadn't known, or hadn't been willing to discuss. Gunderson was betting on the former.

Derwin stopped breathing. Eyes flew wildly about the room, never settling on anything for long.

Gunderson waited patiently. He was good at that, too.

"He was known in the underworld as the Scarlet Slayer," Derwin finally spoke, a seeming non-sequitur. "A crime lord who had taken to wearing a mask and dressing his men up in matching red uniforms, like they did in those days. Another one of those idiots who got a lot of press and even gave interviews, rather than trying to be so quiet nobody knew about them."

He fell silent, introspective, and Gunderson sat back to sip his coffee.

"It's hard, Gunderson," Derwin finally admitted. "Even after all these years."

"What happened?"

"We got a tip, Gunderson," he continued. "Miss Lynx always signed them a particular code that was never known outside a small group of us, to let us know that it was her. She had broken into my files and solved the case before we even knew what the Slayer had planned, so she told us where to go and when."

Gunderson nodded. Again, back to bits and pieces Flanagan had shared.

"The museum is gone now, but at the time it had a small, prestigious collection of arcane artifacts, some of which actually had power," Derwin said.

"Egyptian," Gunderson agreed. "Lot of ancient things dug up that had been lost for a long time, but still worked."

"Exactly," Derwin replied, eyes lighting up like a man who has just seen a life preserver hit the water near his hands as he was about to go under for good. "She had figured out that Slayer was going to break into the place to steal a particular amulet. Someone in her network of underworld spies had let her know, I suppose."

"Who got there first?" Gunderson asked.

"Miss Lynx did, but she was in hiding," Derwin said. "We arrived and came in the front door to catch Scarlet Slayer and his men in the act. All was going well until the Scarlet Slayer decided to play his trump card. He had a bomb, Gunderson. Eight sticks of dynamite that would have blown the place apart. He threw them at us and then started to run. That was when Miss Lynx leapt into action, but in the chaos and confusion, she ended up tossing the bomb out of the wrong window. The building shielded those of us inside, but Scarlet Slayer and most of his men were killed in the parking lot."

He fell silent then.

Gunderson could see the situation. In the comic books, things like that always magically worked out, mostly because the writers were at pains to have the bad guys get away, in order that they could come back later and threaten the hero again and again in later issues.

But Gunderson had been in Africa, and later in Britain and then France. The Army had taught him that *SNAFU* was the normal order of things and that rarely did it all come together for the final splash page.

"That wasn't all of it, was it?" Gunderson pressed, to keep the man's story running because he could sense there was more.

Flanagan had stopped there, but apparently he hadn't known any more than that. But Charles wasn't done, from the look in his eyes.

"It was not," Derwin sighed. His mouth opened and closed a few times, but no words came out at first. "Later, Miss Lynx appeared in my office, at my house, and unmasked herself. She was feeling the guilt for the deaths of those men, and needed someone to talk to."

Gunderson waited. Derwin sipped his coffee.

"I was terribly upset at her for killing those men, detective," he finally continued in a smaller voice. "And I was drunk and maudlin at the stupid loss. Heroes never killed people, you know."

One hand came up defensively to stop whatever conversation he thought Gunderson was about to interject. Or to perhaps ward off a blow.

"That doesn't excuse what I did," he said, angry now, but only at himself. And maybe his ghosts.

Gunderson wondered if Derwin even saw him as anything but a ghost now. One of many, from the look in the man's eyes. He certainly wasn't focused on Gunderson.

"We argued and I struck her, Gunderson, damned fool that I was," Derwin continued. "Knocked that silly mask right out of her hands, but I still didn't see her as my daughter. You see? I only saw the mask. The woman and not my child under it. I screamed at her for murdering those men, even though she hadn't. She tried to walk away and I grabbed at her in my rage. Her costume tore open, showing me all of the beautiful woman. I lost myself and grabbed her. She tried to stop me, but I struck her again and again, finally beating her into submission. And then, God help me…"

Gunderson waited, one of many ghosts circling the man. The rest were probably looking for his blood or soul, but Gunderson just wanted answers. If he allowed himself any emotions at this moment, he'd probably end up beating his own client to death.

He considered doing it anyway.

"I did things to her that night that I have regretted ever since," Derwin said. "Terrible things because her nudity and my anger had caused me to lose control. It's never happened again."

Which left the presumption that perhaps it happened more than once before then.

Gunderson could see the rape in the man's eyes. The violence. Twenty-two-year-old daughter, still living at home and presumably a student at one of the local colleges. Maybe studying to be a cop herself if she managed it. It might have been possible in those days, for the daughter of a senior detective who was good enough.

"She never spoke to me again, Gunderson," Derwin said. "When I woke up in the morning, hungover, she had left her bloody clothes right there on the floor of my office, packed a few things, and vanished."

"But she came back in '42," Gunderson probed, pushing the man forward before he stopped talking and surrendered to his ghosts. "Flanagan said that she returned to active duty after Pearl Harbor, and stayed until V-E Day."

"Yes, but I had retired by then," Derwin said. "Guilt. I tried to contact her but she ignored me. And she had changed. Flanagan was in his prime in those days and worked with her some, without ever knowing that she was my daughter, or what I had done to her. She had gotten brutal and dark."

"And that's the secret the blackmailer threatened to release?" Gunderson asked. "Can I read the letter they sent?"

"Just a moment," Derwin said, and rose, carefully putting his coffee down and disappearing down a hallway.

Gunderson blew out a heavy breath. Apparently, even Flanagan hadn't known the whole truth. Only that his old partner and mentor needed help.

How the hell had he ended up being the one drawn in?

Derwin returned a moment later and handed Gunderson an envelope. The contents had been typed, so there wasn't much that he could do about handwriting, but if they found the machine, that would go a long ways towards identifying the blackmailer. Wasn't much to go on. Just the threat to reveal all the dark secrets of his family if money wasn't forthcoming and a warning that more letters would be coming with more information.

Gunderson expected that the second one would include the usual threat about not going to the cops, but it was missing here, so he presumed that this person wasn't a professional. They usually had certain standards, after all.

He studied Derwin now.

"I know they say that you should never pay a blackmailer, because that just inspires them to keep at it," Derwin said. "They haven't even told me how much, but I have money in the bank. Significant, because of some inheritances, as well as saving from living even more frugally than my pension required."

"It's Wednesday, has the mail arrived yet today?" Gunderson asked.

"No, he usually comes fairly late in the day on his regular route," Derwin said. "Should I contact you directly when the next letter comes?"

"Yes," Gunderson said.

He handed the man a card and got Derwin's phone number so that he could call here and check in, although more than likely he would be working this one through Flanagan.

Gunderson found himself back in the Mallory pretty quickly, pulling away from the curb and automatically watching for trouble. Mostly, he wanted to be far enough away from Derwin that he didn't feel like shooting the man.

This was one of the worst kinds of cases. Nothing good ever came of airing out a family's dirty laundry. The only upside Gunderson could ever see was was perhaps the lives that would be ruined in those cases would people who had it coming.

Charles Derwin, LAPD, retired, was certainly in that category. Gunderson wondered if Emily Derwin still lived anywhere around here. The letter had been mailed from Los Angeles, rather than someplace like Seattle or New York, so his blackmailer was in the area. Maybe even keeping watch on Charles, down here in Orange County.

Gunderson headed north and let the details simmer in the back of his mind.

GUNDERSON DIDN'T REALLY CARE that he was working for LAPD as a client on this one. Nobody in their right mind trusted that organization to keep secrets when there were lives to be destroyed or money to be made from leaking information to the press. Any questions he asked inside the building were going to be echoed outside even before he made it back to his car.

Instead, he went down to the library and spent a couple of hours looking up that decade of costumed superheroes that had been so big and vibrant when he'd been a young punk. Something about Prohibition had taken all the craziness of the Depression and run with it.

Corrupt police departments everywhere hadn't helped, because once people got a taste for bribery and lawlessness over booze, it had been hard getting them to obey other laws. Things had snowballed, at least until Pearl Harbor changed the world in the States.

But the era was over, near as he could tell. Sure, there were still a few of them still around, either those same folks in silly costumes twenty years later still doing it, or a new generation coming along. Except that these days, everyone was much more patriotic. The government had cracked down hard on vigilantes after the war. Leaned on everyone they could find and given them the stark choice of working for the government or being hounded out of business.

Too many other problems going on these days as the Ruskies got over all the crap Stalin had done and the Red Chinese were feeling their oats. Ike was a patient guy, but Gunderson always wondered when Korea would ramp up to crazy again. Or maybe China and Siberia. Or India.

But the government putting all those other yahoos in colorful outfits out of business also meant more business for him as a simple PI. He could live with fewer people running around in tights.

Miss Lynx had been a product of another era in that way.

Born Emily Derwin in 1914, although none of the official records knew that. All they knew was that she appeared in 1932 with a splash, disappeared cold in '36, and then returned in '42 before vanishing forever in '45, after helping fight Nazi fifth columnists and Aryan superheroes that Gunderson suspected were mostly a mix of German officers with a mission and American gangsters with a change of fashion.

Not everyone had listened to the Mob Bosses when those folks announced that they were going to protect the ports from enemy agents until the war was over.

But he didn't need to know that history. He'd lived with a lot of those folks firsthand as an MP. Miss Lynx was his target.

Gunderson wondered if Emily had left L.A. in '36. Lot of folks would have. But to have spent the war years back meant that she had most likely returned. Hopefully, she had remained afterwards.

He wondered what a forty-one year old Emily Derwin would be like. He'd gotten a few pictures of her from her dad. Keepsakes that he was having duplicated.

The Mallory rolled to the curb as Gunderson arrived and he made his way into the newspaper building via an alley entrance to the building that important people didn't generally know existed. A couple of folks nodded as he went by, but nobody spoke. It was midday and they were all running crazy right now trying to put out the afternoon edition.

Gunderson was fine with that. With any luck at all, none of this would even echo inside the building.

He made his way down to the basement. Through a couple of doors to the big vault where the air was kept as cool and dry as possible so old paper and ink didn't fade. The paper had been around for decades at this point, and they were only slowly catching up with getting the old stuff into film for long-term storage.

The entire area was file cabinets. Six feet tall with boxes of crap piled on top of them.

Gunderson found O'Hanlon right where he expected. Feet up. Second bottle of root beer tipped back to keep him from drying out. Master of his domain and probably a complete stranger to the important folks up at the top of the building.

O'Hanlon squinted at him as Gunderson walked close.

"I'm not going to like it, am I?" he asked.

Gunderson grinned.

"You never do," Gunderson said as he took the only chair on this side of the desk and sat. "But I got a bribery budget on this case, and the folks supplying it would shit themselves if they knew it was going to you."

One caustic eyebrow went up and the bottle went down. O'Hanlon had been with the paper for something like forty years at this point. Liked to joke that they put him in the basement and THEN built a building on top of him.

Chubby and pale from hardly ever emerging into the California sun, he had also been accused of being a vampire.

Gunderson had met a few of those folks and they tended to dress better, given the option.

Rumpled, that described O'Hanlon. Red hair finally retreated to mostly bald and faded to white now. Freckles on his skull. Reading glasses, but he was still a shark with a camera, if you wanted a picture taken perfectly.

"Who's paying?" O'Hanlon asked, wiping the back of a hand across his mouth and lifting his feet from the desk.

Man needed to see a cobbler about his right sole.

"They have badges," Gunderson smiled.

"*Do they now?*"

Oh yeah, he had O'Hanlon's undivided attention.

Gunderson slipped a fin across the desk and watched it disappear into a pocket as a really evil grin came across the man's face.

"I need some background," Gunderson explained. "Been to the library and got the public stuff. Want to get deep into the sorts of things that never get printed, and then maybe have you raid some old files for duplicate pictures I might slip out with."

"How bad is it?" O'Hanlon asked.

"Maybe I buy you an early dinner right now?" Gunderson replied.

"Shit, I was afraid of that," he said. Then he finished off his root beer and stood up, turning towards the endless stack of file cabinets that surrounded them. "Jimmy! I'll be back in an hour if anybody needs me."

Someone, maybe Jimmy, yelled something back, and the two of them were ascending those concrete back stairs. Out to the Mallory and into traffic.

"Not even safe enough to eat at one of the local joints?" O'Hanlon asked as Gunderson drove away.

Gunderson shrugged. The windows were down but he didn't figure anybody close by at an intersection would understand.

"I'm looking for a vigilante named Miss Lynx," Gunderson said as he wove closer to the port, where the restaurants were a little rougher, as was the clientele, but no reporters would likely be around to sniff.

"Shit, that's an old name," O'Hanlon grunted. "They find her dead or something? Or is someone looking to out her in retirement and mess up her life?"

"Just about exactly the opposite," Gunderson replied. "She comes in tangential to my case, but I don't know if she is involved. Hoping someone can introduce me to her quietly enough and I can clear her from my list."

"Well, she was the shit when I was still a reporter shooting film," O'Hanlon said. "Body just made to be worshiped by a camera as she did her thing. Vanished for a few years before the war, then came back. Don't think I've heard anything in a decade, not counting the regular *'Whatever happened to…?'* articles that they put up on the editorial page occasionally when the suits want to complain about kids these days."

They shared a grin about a joke as old as Socrates.

"Interested in the war years," Gunderson said as he pulled up next to the diner he wanted.

Mom and Pop kind of place mostly specializing in Italian food, but Americanized by the war. Simple stuff. Peasant food, his mother would have called it, but not in a bad way. Pastas in sauces, with meat. Pizzas of various options. It also happened to be the sort of thing O'Hanlon would really enjoy. If you wanted the man to talk, you dropped a boat of lasagna in front of him, and maybe a little red wine.

"Crap, you're serious," O'Hanlon laughed as they walked up to the front door.

"For you, only the best," Gunderson laughed back. "And I'm not paying."

They got seated and taken care of. Once they were left alone, O'Hanlon turned serious.

"During the war, she was different than she had been," he said. "I want to say darker, but it was the same costume. The same woman. What do you want to know? What can I fill in?"

"Darker?" Gunderson asked.

"Early Lynx just captured the bad guys," O'Hanlon grimaced. "When she came back during the war, she was a lot more trigger happy, killing Nazis, Jap agents, and punks in costumes.

"I know she was young," Gunderson said. "Details that came up suggest she was in her late twenties when the war came."

"Wow, so she was like eighteen when she started?" O'Hanlon was shocked.

"Something like that," Gunderson remained evasive.

The waitress brought a carafe of red and two glasses, but Gunderson was happy to have a short glass and call it good. Bread and olive oil arrived as well.

"So I seem to remember that she had a boyfriend or something during the war," O'Hanlon continued, swirling his glass as Gunderson got into the bread. "Navy guy assigned to the docks who was almost a damsel in distress kind of thing. Don't remember without digging into my files, but we might be able to track down a name."

Dinner passed companionably as O'Hanlon dug into that incredible memory and brought up all sorts of details. Gunderson almost felt like he had read forty or sixty issues of a Miss Lynx comic book by the time they got back to the newspaper and snuck into the basement again.

In through the stacks, O'Hanlon led him into a corner that was separated off by a cyclone fence and a padlock.

Gunderson raised an eyebrow.

"Vigilante section," he said. "Gotta keep it isolated so collectors and fans don't sneak in to steal anything. If they wore a mask, I've got them here. Including that Scarlet Slayer fellow you were asking about."

Gunderson waited while the other man worked. A handful of pictures appeared.

"Don't have hardly anything on the Slayer," O'Hanlon announced, disappointed. "Gotta couple of old-timers upstairs we might hassle if it turns out to be important, but he's dead so I doubt anybody cared enough. And here are a couple of action stills and a publicity photo from the war bonds thing she did in '44."

Gunderson studied the picture. Definitely Emily. A decade older now from the pictures Charles had of her. Growing into an adult body, with curves and a chest now where she'd almost been a waif before, but a lot of that had been acrobatics and gymnastics when she was just a kid.

She wore a mask, but he could see what a decade had done from her high school pictures. Worn, sure, but angry. Maybe he was reading something into it, but Gunderson relied on his instincts, and this was a woman dragged back into doing her thing after she thought she had put behind her forever.

"Oh, almost forgot," O'Hanlon said, handing Gunderson a typed piece of paper. "Got a name on your Navy guy. Lt Commander Hollis Reed. Got a few details on him up to the end of the war, but when she went away, he did, too, so we didn't bother tracking."

Gunderson nodded and thanked the man as he slipped everything into a manila envelope and made his way back up to the street. O'Hanlon had gotten most of the wine in him so he probably hadn't even realized what he'd said.

Gunderson didn't feel like enlightening the man. He needed to talk to some folks.

GUNDERSON FELT like he was doing a jigsaw puzzle in the dark, but that was nothing new in this business. And it was the reason folks hired him to do things. To *know* things.

More importantly, to know people. The key to being a private detective wasn't chasing down bad guys or solving crimes. Usually, it involved finding the right person and asking them the right question.

Right now, that meant someone he had served with as an MP during the war. Dave was still in, going for his twenty. Or maybe thirty. Gunderson wasn't entirely sure. He didn't know if Dave was sure.

They met at a bar around the corner from Dave's office as a recruiter. It was an easy gig for the man. Show up, look good, talk a good game when kids walked through the door. Beat the hell out of serving in South Korea or West Germany.

Gunderson was at the bar, seated near the far end with one empty chair beyond him and a glower that suggested anyone wanting to join him was in for trouble. The place had a tiki theme going, South Pacific, like maybe it was a navy joint, but the locals were colorful enough. The usual Thursday mid-afternoon drunks and a bartender who had been a little surly until Gunderson tipped him a fin and a smile.

It felt good, burning dirty money from the department for a righteous cause. All Flanagan had asked for was a running total of how much was being spent, over and above Gunderson's usual expenses, for reimbursement. No questions about where or what.

Dave walked in and slipped onto the stool at the end, next to Gunderson, dressed like a recruiting poster. It was a little jarring to see, considering what a slob Dave had been during the war, but Gunderson supposed that the lucky ones had found their calling after the war and stuck with it.

He wasn't a cop anymore, but he'd found a thing. At least for now.

Gunderson put a couple of bucks on the bar and ordered a second beer for him and one for Dave. They sipped like old buddies.

"So what brings Gunderson in from the darkness, anyway?" Dave asked after an appreciative sip.

"Ghost hunting," Gunderson replied vaguely.

"Oh?"

"Got a name," he said. "Some relevant details. Hoping I could bribe you to put him through your system and come back with anything. He was an officer during the war. Navy boy. Got a client who lost track of him after VJ-Day and wanted to catch up. Had nowhere else to turn so he hired me."

Dave nodded. Not necessarily the sharpest tool in the shed, but a damned good guy.

"Shouldn't be a problem," Dave said after a moment. "Might take a while, depending, but we can always see what we know."

Gunderson slid him over an envelope that had five bucks in it, as well as copies of what O'Hanlon had found. For most civilians, it would have been a dead end. Most PIs as well, Gunderson guessed.

They chatted for a bit, but they had been ships passing in the night for a decade, so it was mostly just bits and details about folks they had both known. Gunderson told a few stories about some of his cases, details left vague to generally protect the guilty. Dave appreciated them.

Gunderson found himself back at the office, almost at loose ends. The phone rang. He grabbed it before Annabelle did.

"Gunderson."

"A second envelope has arrived, Mr. Gunderson," Charles Derwin spoke quietly. "This one warned me not to talk to the police and told me to be home on tomorrow afternoon, Friday it said, for a phone call that would have details. What do I do?"

"Read me the letter, Mr. Derwin," Gunderson replied,

grabbing a tablet and a pencil from his drawer and starting to write furiously.

Not much more than that, after Derwin was done. More threats to reveal his darkest secrets if he didn't come up with money, without mentioning what secrets those might be.

Gunderson wondered how many men might be led astray merely by some guilt they had accumulated along the way. He wasn't Catholic, but they had a tendency to pile that sort of thing up over time.

"Should I contact Tobias?" Derwin asked.

"No, you did the right thing, Charles," Gunderson said. "I'll talk to the Captain for you. Do you have a gun in the house?"

"Whatever for, Gunderson?" Derwin was surprised.

"If they want you at the house at a particular time, they might show up in person to make demands, rather than call you," Gunderson said. "Blackmailing is illegal and if they threaten you, you'd be within your rights to shoot them."

"Will you be here?"

"I don't know, Charles," he said. "Let me talk to the Captain. I will call you before lunch tomorrow to check in. I might be in the neighborhood, but not at your house, if you have a problem. Or Flanagan might arrange for a few boys to be close by instead."

"Thank you, Mr. Gunderson," Derwin said brightly. "I'm pleased that you have been able to take time out of your life to handle this for me."

Gunderson got him off the phone quickly and called Flanagan's office, got his secretary, left his name.

The phone rang again almost immediately.

"Gunderson."

"Flanagan," the man said. "Can we talk on the phone?"

"Probably not wise," Gunderson said.

Flanagan named a bar about midway between them. It had a kitchen attached that wasn't half bad.

"Thirty minutes?"

"See you then."

———

GUNDERSON FOUND himself ushered politely into a back room when he arrived at the place. Usually a bad sign, but here it just meant that he and Flanagan could talk privately. Or as privately as possible. The man was still a political cop, with everything that implied.

At least the wine was better here. A carafe of red arrived with fresh bread.

"So I just heard from Charles Derwin," Gunderson began, working his way through the bits that didn't include what the man had done to his own daughter.

If Flanagan didn't know, he didn't need to find out now. Certainly not from a relative stranger.

"So you expect trouble tomorrow?" Flanagan asked when Gunderson got that part done.

Gunderson shrugged.

"Outside chance, at best, I think," he replied. "This feels more like psychological torture of the man, rather than a con job for money. The letters read like they were written by amateurs."

"What aren't you telling me?" the Captain asked, like he could smell a rat.

It was only a small one, but there was no mistaking the odor.

"There are some things I am not at liberty to tell you, Captain," he temporized. "If you'd known them already, you would have told me when this started. If you don't, then it's not my place now."

"Do you know what happened with Emily?" Flanagan asked.

Gunderson grunted but didn't speak.

"He won't tell me," Flanagan continued. "Well, wouldn't in the old days. He might if I pushed now."

"It might not be something you want to know, Flanagan." Gunderson gave as much warning as he felt he could, given the circumstances.

"I know she hated the man later," the Captain said. "Emily disappeared at the same time that Charles took his retirement, but he never told me why, other than that they had quarreled and he was desperately sorry for the things he said to her. Do you suppose she'd behind this? Something she found out and confronted him about?"

"It's possible," Gunderson replied evasively. "I have a lead on her that I'm following up on. Whatever happened to the son? To Gerald Derwin. Of all the things I've heard about Charles and Emily, Gerald's name never comes up."

It was Flanagan's turn to squirm uncomfortably. He even went so far as to take a long drink of the wine, eyes never leaving Gunderson's.

"I can tell you this in confidence, but it needs to remain under the table," Captain Flanagan finally began. Gunderson nodded. "I know your background, Gunderson, so I know you will appreciate the circumstances. Gerry Derwin was a cop like you before the war. Enlisted like so many men of your generation."

Flanagan hesitated now.

"He get killed over there?" Gunderson guessed.

"If only we'd been so lucky," Flanagan sighed. "He came home, but like a lot of men, you included, he wasn't all there. Couldn't handle being a cop, even though we welcomed him back. Stress was too much, so he dove into the bottle and they ended up giving him a partial pension with some medical disability, plus some money from the government. Last five years or so, he's been gone, as far as I know. Too many people around here knew who he was, or what he had become, so he left. Gone without a trace."

Gunderson grunted noncommittally. Gerry might have also known about Emily as Miss Lynx. Or maybe heard what happened that night. Any number of things, but nothing he could say, even to a relatively honest cop.

Flanagan seemed to understand that. He looked Gunderson square in the eyes now.

"Just make sure you call me, when you get down to that final confrontation, okay?" he demanded.

"If I can, Captain," Gunderson promised. "Got a lot of knives in the air right now and no idea which ones are going to cut me."

MORNING.

Gunderson wasn't one of those PIs that drank himself to sleep every night because the job was too much. Maybe he drank a little too much at times, but that was mostly social lubrication, usually with friends, and never alone.

A grown man should never drink alone.

So he had the added benefit of rising with the sun minus the terrible hangover of some of his peers. Or at least competitors. Man drinks that much wasn't a peer, regardless of the ID or badge in his wallet.

Gunderson had his usual breakfast at the diner, with the usual early folks. The first shift workers on the way to make airplanes, from the way a lot of them were dressed. His people.

He made it to the office early as well, but Annabelle was

already there, half hidden behind a sweater she was knitting for a nephew in Texas.

"Dave called," she said from behind the pile of yarn as soon as he walked in the door. "Has a message for you. Please call soonest."

Gunderson thanked her and settled behind his big desk, dialing.

He got Dave on the phone pretty quick.

"So I got good news and bad news," Dave said. "Found your boy, but he was killed by a drunk driver a couple of years ago. Got an address in Pasadena where checks are still sent, if that helps."

Gunderson wrote it all down, thanked the man, and got him off the phone. Spinning, he looked at the various phone books for different cities that he had bought or stolen along the way until he found Pasadena. Wealthy place, growing by leaps and bounds for two generations now, and doing well at it.

Gunderson found the listing for Reed that matched the address he'd been given, but it wasn't for Hollis Reed.

The name listed was simply E. Reed.

Emily Reed (nee Derwin)?

The address didn't look like the sort of place a blackmailer lived. People around there were the sorts of folks who got hit up for money. Still it would take him northeast instead of south. That might be a problem today.

Gunderson dialed, guessing that the old man would be awake.

"Derwin household," the man said when he answered.

"Gunderson," he countered. "Tracking down some leads today. Do you have any friends or relatives in Pasadena?"

"Pasadena?" Derwin exclaimed. "No. Not to the best of my knowledge, Detective. Do you think you've found the person? Should I still be here this afternoon?"

Gunderson checked his watch. Much as he wanted to race around like his hair was on fire, he needed to do this one slowly and carefully. Blackmailers could strike from anywhere, so if you give them any hint that you're onto them, they would just disappear.

Until later.

"I'll call Flanagan and ask him to put a couple of men close by," Gunderson said. "I'm hoping that I'll be able to make it down to Orange County, but I'd rather be safe than sorry. I'll check in after lunch."

"That would be marvelous, Gunderson," Derwin said, brightening. "I look forward to it."

Gunderson hadn't even gotten his hat off, so he put the phone book back and headed out to the front office. Flanagan wouldn't be in the office for a bit, so he'd call from someplace on the road.

"Annabelle, I'm on a lead, but I have a lot of irons in the fire," he said to her. "Can you stay a little late if I need you to? I can have some food delivered as well, expensed to the client."

"You go chase down whoever Dave found for you," she smiled. "I can knit here just as well as at home or at the senior center."

He nodded and headed out.

Traffic wasn't that bad headed east and then north. Pasadena really was something of a paradise. Enough water that things could be green. Enough money that they would stay that way. Gunderson worked his way inward like a wasp circling a victim.

Nice house. Old craftsman, well maintained. Yard that screamed Japanese gardener, although these days it was probably a nice Mexican family that came by once a week and committed art.

Gunderson parked on the far side of a tree-lined street

and got out, hat on his head as a statement of officialness or something. He had his Smith .44 under his arm inside the green suit, but doubted that he would need it. Not many people as tall and big as him. Plus he'd learned fisticuffs from drunk marines. Or taught it, maybe.

He rang the bell and straightened his tie.

The door behind the screen opened and Gunderson gasped. Just a little. Hardly audible.

She still noticed. Her whole face squinted a little, brows hooding like a hungry hawk. The hair was shoulder length and only golden to midway now, with gray roots showing where she hadn't bothered dying them. Well-dressed woman in a white shirt and dark slacks.

Mrs. Reed was still as beautiful as she had been in 1932 when she had been Emily Derwin.

"Yeah?" she asked in a quiet, hard voice, like she had already figured out who he was and was just about to go all costumed vigilante badass on him as he stood on the porch.

Gunderson didn't trust his voice, so he held out a card with just the tips of his fingers.

She slipped the door open just enough to grasp it and then retreated a half step. Enough that she could still slam the door in his face if she chose.

"What do you want, Gunderson?" she said after a moment. "The past is dead and gone."

"Considering the neighborhood, I'd rather not yell things across the way to you, if folks around here don't already know."

He waited, not inviting himself in, in case she wanted to go to a nearby diner or something. A blackmailer confronted like this would have already either started running or shooting, eight chances in ten, but she felt like a housewife. Maybe an ex-superhero.

Not a criminal.

Emily studied his face for a long moment.

"Who hired you?" she asked, voice sharp with pain and anger.

"Technically, the LAPD, although I'm not supposed to say that," he replied quietly. "They'd like to keep things quiet, if possible."

"What the hell do the police want with me?" she demanded in a quiet growl.

"May I come in?" he asked. "Or would it be better if we talked on the porch?"

Another growl, this one wordless, and she pushed the screen open, stepping well back and leading him to a front room that had the appearance of a stage set. Pretty, but hardly ever used. The place you would entertain guests that you didn't know all that well, rather than inviting them into the back of the house or the back yard for brewskies.

There was money in this room. Matching couch and wingback chair. Coffee table with art books that suggested she had an interest in photography. More books on a case with some plants arranged to make everything softer.

Emily took the chair, so Gunderson perched on the farthest edge of the couch away from her. Nobody suggested coffee, so he took his hat off and sat it beside him, running a hand back through Swedish hair that was probably long enough that he should stop by a barber at some point.

Pretty soon it would start turning gray like hers.

Gunderson drew a heavy breath as the quiet woman watched him. He watched her as well.

Softer than she'd been in pictures taken a decade ago, but she would be forty-one now, and not eighteen. Still in fantastic shape for a woman of any age, but he could see where she'd stopped the ferocious morning calisthenics that someone had to maintain for that level of lithe limberness that a skin-tight costume required.

Glancing around, he caught no hint of children, even though she had married Lt. Commander Reed when she was in her early thirties.

"I'm just going to talk," Gunderson said, making sure that he could see anyone trying to sneak up the hallway at him, even though she felt like a woman who lived alone. "I have a pretty good idea who you were, once upon a time, but it only tangentially impacts on my case."

"Go ahead," Emily prompted him, emotions just about as compact as she could get from what he could see.

"When was the last time you were in contact with your father?" Gunderson asked carefully.

Her face hardened. She was possessed of a rage for the ages, but only for a second and then it passed, like a forge fire banked. The kind that could make swords or immolate the unwary.

Gunderson had uncomfortable images of angry dragons in his head.

"1936," she replied, biting off every syllable with perfect teeth.

Gunderson nodded.

"And you retired for good in 1945, yes?" he pressed ahead. "Married Lt. Commander Reed in completely secrecy once all the war silliness was done and you two could ride off into the sunset together?"

"Something like that."

Again, bitter and angry, but Gunderson got the impression that she'd been expecting him. Well, not him and not today, but that someday, someone would appear on her front porch and knock.

"My condolences on your loss, Mrs. Reed," Gunderson inclined his head. "From what I've seen in the old records, Hollis Reed was a good man."

"He was," she agreed, giving him no more than that.

No emotional hooks that he could grasp onto to soften what was coming. But she'd been a hard woman during the war years.

"As I said, LAPD hired me, under the table, to track someone down," Gunderson said. "Maybe you. Maybe someone else. Someone causing trouble."

He watched, but she had no reaction to his words. No guilt. Maybe a little surprise, like she'd been expecting that knock to be someone like O'Hanlon with a camera instead, hoping for an interview.

"Charles Derwin has been getting letters, Mrs. Reed," Gunderson just went ahead and said it. "Blackmail threats, to tell the world all his dark secrets if money wasn't forthcoming."

There. That was true rage. Pure and white hot.

She muttered something under her breath that sounded suspiciously like *fucker has is coming."* but he couldn't be sure. Didn't doubt it, though. Tended to agree with her.

"He might," Gunderson agreed anyway. "But blackmail is still a crime in this town, and the police would like it squashed like a bug."

"Surprised that old shit is still alive, Gunderson," she said now, softening down from the wrath of the gods themselves to maybe something a biblical prophet might have brought home with him from a month on a mountaintop.

"As I understand it, Charles Derwin retired from the police department in 1936, Mrs. Reed," Gunderson said. "Tobias Flanagan was the one who hired me when Charles Derwin contacted him about this issue."

Gunderson was careful not to call the man her father now. Looking at her face, she didn't have a father.

But there was also something different in her eyes now. Childhood crush on Tobias Flanagan? Maybe. The man was about a decade older than her, so he would have been in his prime when she was doing her thing. But he'd also been Charles Derwin's partner. Couldn't forget that.

"Do you own a typewriter, Mrs. Reed?" he asked out of the blue.

The best way to entrap someone is to whipsaw them with emotions and confusion. Worked here, as her face went completely blank for nearly a second.

"What are you talking about?" she sputtered, confused rather than enraged.

"The letters were typed, Mrs. Reed," he replied. "If you own one, I'd like to get a sample of writing from it. That either incriminates you or clears you."

"I don't have one," she said. "Hollis never brought his work home with him and I prefer writing letters longhand."

Gunderson imagined that she had a fantastic hand, as beautiful as everything else was about the woman.

"If I could see your office, it would help, Mrs. Reed."

Blue eyes. All the old photos had been black and white, so they hadn't captured how vibrantly alive her eyes were. They focused on him now and threatened to turn him to stone if he wasn't careful.

She watched him for a long moment, not breathing.

"Why are you here, Gunderson?" she finally asked. "As opposed to sending cops, if you think I did it."

"I don't think you did."

"Really?"

"I'm trying to prove that the dog didn't bark, Mrs. Reed," Gunderson apologized now. "There isn't a more difficult task in my line of work."

She nodded at that and rose, so he did as well, grabbing his hat and keeping his distance as she walked back to the hallway and stopped next to an open door, turning to block him from what was obviously her bedroom at the end.

Gunderson stopped as far away from her as he could,

staying on this side of the frame and only leaning to look in the room. Office, but such as a man would have done it, with wood paneling and a couple of big, metal file cabinets like the ones Gunderson kept in his office. Pictures of Hollis Reed over the last twenty-five years and Emily Derwin-Reed from the last decade or so. Knick-knacks. Open, rolltop desk along one wall. Nothing at all like a typewriter.

"Satisfied?" she growled from close.

Gunderson withdrew his head to keep the doorway between them before turning to study her.

Tall for a woman. Maybe five-nine or five-ten. Still small next to him, but most women were.

"Thank you," he said simply, trying not to roil things even more than he had.

Gunderson withdrew now, but only as far as that front room. He sat again on the couch and waited for her to return to the chair.

"I'm willing to concede, on the surface of things, that you aren't involved, Mrs. Reed," he said carefully. "Who else might know about that night?"

She flinched, but he'd been expecting that. There was no easy way to approach that topic.

He watched all the layers peel off as it came to the surface again, but then she shoved it all to one side in her mind as he studied her eyes. The crime fighter awoke from her long slumber and came to the fore.

It was like a different woman suddenly inhabited the flesh in a bizarre, eerie manner.

"Mrs MacGillicuty had gone home for the evening," Miss Lynx said now. "She was the cook and maid. I only went to talk to—…my father because she had left. Gerry, my brother, was out with some friends, probably at a drug store having a sundae knowing him. We were alone. I felt safe enough. Had felt safe enough. That was obviously untrue."

Gunderson nodded rather than talk. Miss Lynx was back, possibly for the first time in a decade. And he was forcing her to relive the worst night of her entire life. Her voice had dropped to a hard growl more suited to a man.

"After he passed out on top of me, I managed to get out from under that drunk," Emily recalled slowly, angrily. "There was blood everywhere, Gunderson. Mine, because I had been a virgin until then."

Gunderson growled quietly, but held his peace. He needed to solve Charles Derwin's current problem, before he decided what to do about the older one.

"My main costume was destroyed, so I left it, grabbing all my hidden spares and some other clothes," she continued. "I had a lot of money saved up from rewards and bounties. Didn't take much of anything else. Walked out the door and never spoke with the man again."

"He said he tried to contact you during the war," Gunderson spoke carefully.

"Through Flanagan," she nodded. "I ignored everything. Letters Tobias wanted to give me got thrown in his face without explanation. Hollis was the only one who knew how to reach me during those days, but he didn't ever find out the truth."

"What did you do after you left?" Gunderson asked, mostly trying to fill in gaps in the story, but he was a man who was all about solving puzzles.

"Went to Tijuana for a time," she said quietly.

"Tijuana?"

"I had a problem after that drunkard raped me, Gunderson," she snarled. "So I had to go someplace where I could take care of it. But they botched the job, and so I could never have children after that. Hollis didn't care and loved me for me."

Gunderson nodded. Yeah, TJ would be the best place for

those sorts of doctors, for a young, unwed woman with money, who wanted to keep things secret. Especially if her father was a relatively famous cop up in Los Angeles.

"For a couple of years, I just knocked around under a fake name," Miss Lynx continued. "I'd prepared something for eventually moving out and still retaining my costumed identity, so I was just her for a while."

"Did you work?"

"I had a lot of money, Gunderson," she retorted. "Insurance companies paid well for recovering valuable artifacts. Gangsters always had rewards posted for their capture. All of that had gone into a bank and a variety of investments. I studied finance in college. Hollis had a retirement from the Navy, as well as rewards I had accumulated from the war days. Plus Hollis had a life insurance policy I had been hoping to never cash."

Again, he nodded. Looking around, the whole house spoke of old money, but it still felt like an empty, hollow place.

"So you were her during the War as well?" he asked, just to finish filling in gaps.

Miss Lynx nodded.

"I haven't bothered looking up the marriage license, or I would know who you had been in those days," he observed carefully. "Right now I don't suppose it matters. I might be in touch, depending on how the case progresses, but I don't think I need to bother you for now, Mrs. Reed."

He rose, and the uncostumed Miss Lynx did as well, seeing him to the door. Emily wasn't there. In her place, a crime fighter stood menacingly.

"I can't say I'm interested in what happens to that shit, Gunderson," she said carefully. "But I'd like to hear how it all turns out, when this is all over."

"I'll see what I can do, Mrs. Reed," he said.

"Miss Lynx," she corrected him in a sharp voice, but he knew that was coming.

"Miss Lynx," he agreed and saw himself to the car.

He made it as far as a corner drug store and located a phone booth in the parking lot. Checking the time, it was a little past one, but he could go a while before he worried about lunch. He dialed Charles Derwin instead.

"Hello?"

"Gunderson, Mr. Derwin," he said. "Any news?"

"Yes, Mr. Gunderson," the man said in an almost excited voice. "He just called a few minutes ago."

"He?" Gunderson confirmed. "It was a man's voice?"

"It was."

"Did you recognize it at all?" Gunderson pressed.

Gerry Derwin was still an option, even if Gunderson had serious doubts about Emily. Doubly so as he'd just been at her house, probably during the time the phone call was occurring. She would have had more of an emotional reaction, had she been involved.

"I did not, Gunderson," Derwin replied. "It was a deep, quiet kind of voice, possibly with something of an Irish accent, but I might have imagined it."

"What did he say?"

"That I needed to pay him five thousand dollars, cash, tonight, or he would contact the press with all the sordid details of my misdeeds, Mr. Gunderson." Charles said. "He warned me not to call the cops or to have anyone follow me tonight when I brought him the money, or bad things would happen."

"You haven't called the police, Charles," Gunderson reminded him, "I'm a private citizen. Did he tell you where you would meet him?"

"No, he said he would be watching the house and would call me when I got home from the bank."

Gunderson considered the situation. It was doubtful that the man would be watching the house. Too easy to stand out. But he could easily find a vantage point to watch the bank this afternoon without being obvious.

"Charles, I want you to go to the bank like he demanded," Gunderson said. "Take a briefcase or something with you, but only withdraw one hundred dollars and then come straight home and wait for him to call. Keep your gun with you, just in cast. Flanagan can back up the story if someone sees it and wants to arrest you. I need to make some stops and check things, then I will call you in a few hours."

"Very good, Mr. Gunderson."

BACK TO THE NEWSPAPER.

Down the back stairs and into the morgue. O'Hanlon was still there, always there. Feet up. Cold bottle of root beer handy. Worn sole.

"More?" he asked as Gunderson emerged from the stacks.

"Specific question, but you'll have to look it up for me and you were on my way where I was going," Gunderson replied.

"Shoot." O'Hanlon rose, grabbing his bottle as he did. "Back to the cage?"

Gunderson nodded and followed.

Inside, O'Hanlon turned and looked at him expectantly.

"The Scarlet Slayer file," Gunderson said. "I seem to remember something you mentioned over dinner, but need to double check it."

O'Hanlon moved to a cabinet and opened it, withdrawing a thin file and laying it on a handy table.

"Most of the crime in this town in the old days was

Italian, right?" Gunderson asked. "At least until the Okies started showing up?"

"Correct," O'Hanlon replied. "A few gangs came north from places like Ensenada or Acapulco, but they generally were just suppliers. Only once you got farther inland, to places in the Inland Empire and Riverside, would there be Mexican gangs, but they were mostly folks who already lived here when whites started showing up. Part of the landscape, as it were."

"What about the Irish?" Gunderson asked.

"A lot of them ended up being cops, Gunderson," O'Hanlon laughed. "Or old newspaper hounds like me."

"What about Scarlet Slayer?" Gunderson asked.

"He's dead, Gunderson," O'Hanlon said. "You think that your problems were part of his gang?"

"Nobody ever found the man's body, O'Hanlon," Gunderson retorted.

Rather than answer, the man turned and studied the file closely.

"I'll be a son of a…"

O'Hanlon looked up.

"I saw it earlier," Gunderson confirmed. "Plus I've been talking to people who were there."

"The cops?"

"And Miss Lynx," Gunderson said quietly.

"Shit, she's still around?" O'Hanlon gasped.

"She is, but she doesn't want to talk to a reporter."

"I can be very persuasive," O'Hanlon smiled.

"I have to solve this case first," Gunderson growled at the man to keep him on track.

"So you're right, Gunderson," O'Hanlon admitted. "The bomb went out the window and blew up the car where Scarlet Slayer and his men were starting to drive away. Blew it all to hell, but nobody ever saw the man again, so they assumed he'd been blown to bits by the dynamite."

"What if he'd escaped?"

"Why wait twenty years for revenge?" O'Hanlon asked.

"Maybe he was nearly killed and had to recover, O'Hanlon," Gunderson suggested. "Derwin retired immediately afterwards, so maybe it took the man this long to locate him. I know Derwin had been living a quiet life since then, down out of the way in Orange County. Could Scarlet Slayer still be alive?"

"Sure," O'Hanlon said. "They never recovered a body they could identify as him. Of course, you're overlooking another good comic book trope here. Literature uses it, too."

"What's that?"

"Maybe we're dealing with a kid that had to grow up before he could start on his quest for revenge?" O'Hanlon asked. "Lots of times in the old stories, you had to wait a generation for that sort of thing. If Slayer was killed, or seriously disabled, maybe he had a kid who had to come of age?"

"I'll let you know, O'Hanlon," Gunderson said. "Pretty sure that it will all come out in the next few days."

"I'm not going to get anything else out of you, am I?"

"Monday, maybe you can buy me dinner," Gunderson smiled.

NIGHTFALL.

Flanagan's two cops had quietly stayed near Derwin all day and not seen anything, but Gunderson presumed that whoever was watching wasn't completely incompetent. Rookie, maybe, but not dumb. Never assume they were dumb.

Whoever it was hadn't tapped Derwin's phone, either, hopefully, or they would have known about a PI running around.

Gunderson was down at an all-night diner close to the beach, reading the afternoon paper and having a sandwich while he waited. Derwin would call the payphone next to Gunderson when he was ready to leave the house.

The instructions had said a spot on the docks themselves, down in all those warehouses where you could get lost easily. Or sneak up on someone just as easily.

Gunderson hadn't shared his theories with Derwin or Flanagan. O'Hanlon had only been guessing and nobody would know until it all went down. On the brighter side, Gunderson didn't have to worry about the cops getting pissy if he did end up shooting a blackmailer tonight. It would be listed as self-defense on the reports Flanagan would file. That much he had already been told.

Gunderson had even momentarily considered calling Emily Reed and inquiring if Miss Lynx wanted to come out for one last adventure. Widow. Retired costumed vigilante. Anything was possible.

But he didn't know how she would react to Charles Derwin and really didn't need that extra complication in his case. Monday, maybe, he'd tell her about all this and find out what a beautiful woman like that intended to do with the rest of her life.

Forty-one was too young to shut yourself in and grow old. Gunderson was only a few years younger and had to remind himself of that from time to time. For him, too easy to get lost in the job.

The phone beside him rang and Gunderson grabbed it quickly.

"Gunderson."

"Charles Derwin," he said and then hung up immediately.

The clock had started. Summer meant that the night didn't really start until after nine, and it was a Friday, so folks would be out for having fun. That just meant a lot of traffic for him to hide in while watching to see if he had any tails.

If they existed, they were good, as he circled a few times without seeing anyone and eventually ended up close to the place where Derwin was supposed to meet with the blackmailer. Not too close, because he didn't want to give the game away, but close enough that he had to be sneaky.

The Mallory got parked and Gunderson started his stalk, like he was back in the Army trying to get the drop on a couple of punks sneaking out after dark to party off base. The area was warehouses, some big, some small, but a couple of blocks from the waterfront itself, so things were quieter here.

Any closer to the water and you'd have trucks and people coming and going constantly, which Gunderson doubted the blackmailer wanted. Still, he was close enough that the man could easily take the money, kill Charles Derwin, and then flee to a boat nearby, where he could get out three miles pretty fast and then maybe make his way south of the border.

A lot of booze and later narcotics had come and gone the same way over the years.

The meet was going to be done indoors, which made sense. Easier to control the perimeter. Harder for folks to see things from any distance or eavesdrop.

The building itself looked half-abandoned, but Gunderson wasn't fooled. He'd seen too many places like this in Seattle, once upon a time, and other places. You didn't want it looking too impressive, same you didn't want it looking like a dump. Maybe a business that had suffered a run of bad luck and closed up shop for a few days or weeks while bankers rearranged things under new owners. Gunderson smiled as he approached from the blind side.

He found a fire door that was closed and locked, off an alleyway not much wider than a single truck. Out came the lockpicks and it only took him a few moments to get it to surrender.

Dark outside, so he was careful opening it, but the interior of the place was dim as well. Perfect.

Gunderson slid in and closed the door as silently as possible, looking around. The exterior might look bad, but the inside told a story of business moving briskly, with crates and stacks and things. There were a few lights over yonder, but nothing here, so he moved silently, circling to his left.

Somewhere, at least one bay door was open from the sounds of the night coming in. Lights over there marked the spot as well. Presumably the place where Charles Derwin was supposed to arrive, money in hand to buy off a bad man who held secrets too terrible to know.

Not for the first time, Gunderson wondered if maybe the blackmailer had been fishing, and just happened to get a good hit on weak bait. This whole thing could be a junior varsity con man who had gotten lucky. Or it could be the Slayer or his kid come to claim vengeance. He doubted Gerry Derwin and knew it wasn't Emily.

That left the rest of the phone book to hide in.

Little noise as he moved, listening on all sides. Gunderson considered it for a moment then went ahead to bring out the cannon. Smith and Wesson. .44 Magnum. Silver bullets in copper jackets. Real anti-tank gun of a pistol. Man got shot with that and he'd be on his ass trying to figure out what happened as he bled to death. Werewolves, too.

Gunderson normally solved cases with his mind and occasionally with his fists, but tonight felt ugly. Old vengeance twenty years in the making ugly. Vultures coming to roost, and not just chickens.

But LAPD would back up whatever story Gunderson wanted to tell when he was done, so he could afford to play this a little looser than normal.

Life got cold and dark as he settled that widowmaker in his right mitt and shifted from the shadow he was in to another one, closer to his target.

Gunderson could sense them now. A group, but a small one. Boss and a couple of punks, seated just on the other side of a stack of boxes, talking in low voices. Any closer and he'd pop out into the clear where they could see him, but that was fine. He wanted them looking the other way when it dropped.

"He's here," a man's voice said quietly.

The accent had that hard burr of a native Irish speaker. Kind of singsong. Not something easily faked and the man had no reason not to sound like himself right now anyway, so Gunderson finally eliminated Gerry Derwin from his checklist. That just left the rest of the world, at least those that had grown up in Ireland. Or maybe Boston.

Movement sounds as several people slid chairs back from a table and stood. At least one Tommy gun cocking. Those had a specific, peculiar sound. Gunderson had carried one in the war long enough to recognize it, even a decade later. Presumably pistols would be coming out as well.

If a firefight broke out, he'd be in a pinch, but Gunderson reached into his left pocket and touched both speed loaders for luck. Eighteen bullets, and then he would be down to a knife in a pocket and his fists.

Feet as well, because if it got that far, he'd be curb-stomping whoever was left. Maybe should have asked Emily. Or seen if Tobias Flanagan had any special operatives he could have sent.

But Gunderson wanted to do this his way.

A car pulled into the warehouse finally, setting the parking brake as the engine died. A car door opened, then closed a few moments later.

Gunderson hoped that everyone would be watching the other way, so he slid to the edge of the stack of boxes and peeked around.

Four men, facing away, including one wearing a stupid-looking hooded mask in scarlet cloth and a long opera cape.

Seriously? We're back to costumed vigilantes?

But wasn't that what this was all about? Someone wanted to be the Scarlet Slayer.

Or avenge him.

Whether it was the original man, a kid, or someone deciding to mask up and pretend really didn't matter. The FBI had him listed as 'Missing, Presumed Dead' but there was still a reward, dead or alive, all these years later.

Gunderson had checked, on the off chance.

Slayer was unarmed, near as Gunderson could tell. Two punks on the man's right, one of them with the Tommy and the other with a revolver. Long-slide Colt .45 on the left. The punks were all dressed as mugs, rather than in any sort of matching costumes, so presumably this was a one-time thing, rather than the beginning of a new crime spree.

That might be the thing that brought Miss Lynx out of retirement, if the Scarlet Slayer returned from the dead.

Gunderson needed to make sure that that he stayed dead, then.

"Stop right there," Slayer yelled into the distance.

"I've come," Charles Derwin called back calmly. "I brought your money."

"Do you know who I am?" Slayer yelled.

"You're dressed like my old nemesis, the Scarlet Slayer, but the voice is wrong," Derwin answered.

"He's dead, copper." That lilt got heavier now, up and down and across those vowels. "Ye killed 'im. But I'm here to return the favor in the killin' o'yu."

Gunderson smiled. In the movies, your hero always had to provoke a confrontation and get the bad guy to shoot first, somehow missing at short range, so the good guy was defending himself when all else had failed.

Screw that.

Gunderson shot Tommy gun square between the shoulder blades with a roar like an angry dragon waking up.

All hell broke loose.

Slayer bolted for cover. Revolver turned and fired one shot wildly. Long-slide went for cover.

Gunderson shot Revolver next, driving the man over backwards. Two down.

Bullets started impacting the boxes around him, so Gunderson dropped back to cover and started to circle. No way in hell he wanted to play hide and seek in a dark warehouse when everyone had guns. Or rather, they could hide while he hunted them.

More gunfire behind him. Sounded like maybe Derwin had gotten into the act now. Somebody had picked up the Tommy gun and opened up with a sound like a T-Rex-sized woodpecker typing a manifesto in blood.

Elevation to see would be nice, but that was an easy way to get trapped, so he jogged to the end of the current aisle, gun sniffing forward in case anyone else had gotten the same idea. Nobody, so he got there clear and turned to his left.

Across the bottom of the space, he peeked again. Long-slide was firing off to the right, but the distance was too great for Gunderson to trust a shot. Still, he fired one anyway, waited for the man to duck for cover as wood exploded nearby from a crate. He crossed to the next aisle. Derwin and Slayer seemed to be shooting it out somewhere. Hopefully, cop instincts had been good enough for the old man to get behind his car where the engine would protect him some.

Gunderson moved up the next aisle quickly, reaching into his pocket and pulling out the first speed loader. Three down. Three to go. Then six.

The boxes were partly stacked up and partly on shelf units that could be accessed with a fork lift or something, so there were random gaps. Gunderson paid attention to them for movement as he got close.

There. Long-slide was stalking the other direction, possibly thinking that Gunderson was still at the end of that row hiding or something.

Gunderson froze and waiting for the man to cross out of sight of the tiny gap. Then he slipped into that space. Tight, but he could make it work for now.

He squeezed forward until he could see through the boxes. Long-slide was approaching the end of the aisle, where he would discover that Gunderson had circled back on him.

Gunderson got an arm and head into the open and aimed carefully. Two shots, because it was dark and the man was forty feet away. One of them got him. Long-slide collapsed into a puddle of darkness.

Gunderson withdrew into the stack and opened his cylinder, dropping out the one good round with five brass and dumping them into a pocket before reloading six. He turned in place and aimed at the opening he had crawled into, just in case Slayer had seen him.

A moment later, submachinegun fire from his left, so Gunderson crept back out of his hiding spot and looked towards that end of the space.

Things had just gotten ugly.

"I have you now," Slayer screamed as he ran, jumping up the running board and then hood of Derwin's car, firing full auto as he did.

The range was a bit long, so Gunderson put the entire cylinder into the man as fast as he could pull the trigger and control the climb on his muzzle. Something hit square, because Scarlet Slayer tumbled forward over the vehicle, the Tommy gun rattling noisily across the concrete.

Gunderson reloaded as he moved, but he was pretty sure that he was the only person still alive in the warehouse. Man develops a sense for those sorts of things after enough dead bodies.

Still, he was careful as he got close, circling the trunk of Derwin's sedan and ready to empty the rest of his bullets.

Wasn't needed.

Slayer was face-down on the pavement in a pool of blood the same color as his stupid opera cape. Charles Derwin was on his ass, leaned back against the front tire, also covered in blood with his revolver held in one flopped hand that tried to come up until he saw who it was.

"It's done, isn't it?" Charles Derwin asked in a hard wheeze, looking more and more like a tired, old man on his last legs. "You got them all?"

"I did," Gunderson agreed, holstering his pistol now as he walked to the man and squatted.

"I'm done, too, Gunderson," Derwin said tiredly. "The Scarlet Slayer got his revenge."

He paused for a long moment before he continued.

"She won't care, but tell Emily I'm sorry."

"I will," he replied, watching the light go out of Charles Derwin's eyes.

Gunderson felt for a pulse, but that was just automatic. There were at least two wounds on Derwin's chest and there was no way in hell that anyone could get him to a hospital in time to save him. Probably just as well. Saved Gunderson having to think about doing it himself.

They were all dead. Charles Derwin. The Scarlet Slayer.

Even Miss Lynx, when you thought about it. Emily wouldn't put a costume on again. Not in this day and age.

Gunderson walked to the blackmailer and rolled him over onto his back.

Dead as a doorknob. Good riddance.

He pulled the mask off, just so he could see which bet he should have taken with O'Hanlon.

Young face. Maybe twenty-four. Freckles. Orange hair cropped short. Blue eyes already filmed over and blank.

Like O'Hanlon had said, maybe the kid had needed to grow up in order to pursue his revenge. Hopefully, he had remembered to dig two graves when he started out. You always should.

Gunderson stood and looked at the scene one last time, committing it all to memory so O'Hanlon could write up one last supervillain battle for retired Police Lieutenant Charles Derwin, Scourge of the Underworld and a man who had single-handedly taken on a gang of hoodlums and the reborn Scarlet Slayer, returned from the dead.

Lurid as hell, but it would sell papers, and maybe the old man's ghost would gain some solace from it all. At the least the LAPD could mark this case closed. Both cases.

Gunderson pulled the garage door closed after making sure it wasn't locked so he could get back in. There was a payphone a couple blocks over, where he would call Tobias Flanagan and have him send in folks to clean up the mess.

GUNDERSON STUDIED the beautiful woman seated across the diner table from him, sipping her coffee and thinking.

"You expect me to like it, Gunderson?" she demanded in a quiet, angry voice.

"No," he replied, picking up his own mug and finishing it as the waitress came round with the pot. "But I promised a dying man I would do that much."

"Did you promise to make him a hero?" she snapped, holding out her cup as well.

"I did not, Mrs. Reed," Gunderson said firmly. "Any other story I told, however, would have brought you into it somehow. Either of you. Didn't think either of you wanted that, so I had to construct a fable that never mentioned the real reason Derwin retired. Guilt over blowing up Scarlet Slayer and his whole gang makes him sympathetic for the cops and takes all the spotlight off a certain person who also disappeared in 1936 for six years."

"Now what?" she demanded staring coldly at him.

"Now, my case is done," Gunderson replied. "LAPD has everything they need. The blackmailers are all dead. Derwin died enough of a hero for this stupid fairy tale, but he's dead and gone and won't ever bother you again. What you do next is between you and God."

"Really?" she asked dryly. "No advise or suggestions from the invincible Gunderson as to what I should be doing?"

"No, Mrs. Reed," he retorted.

"Emily."

"Emily," he nodded. "The past is buried, both the good and the bad. All you can do is get up tomorrow and make the best of what time you have left. I do what I do because I'm good at it. And maybe I make the world a better place. Derwin and the Slayer are both in hell where they belong, being judged on a scale heavily weighted, I hope."

"What do you think I should do?" Emily asked in a quieter, softer voice now.

Gunderson considered his words carefully before he finally spoke.

"I had considered, briefly, asking if that other you might

want to come that night, but decided that it would be too much of a wildcard, in what was already going to be a messy situation," Gunderson finally told her.

"As you said, Gunderson, she'd dead and buried," Emily said. "Has been since 1945. Why would I want to relive that?"

"You used to be pretty good at the thinking side of the game," Gunderson pointed out, broaching carefully onto the topic. "Most of what I do is put together tidbits until I have a picture, like doing a jigsaw puzzle. A little bit of sneaking, usually when a spouse might be having an affair and I have to get it on film. Gunfights like that one are exceedingly rare. Emily Reed could always become a PI, if she decided she was done living in that quiet house in Pasadena."

"You're insane, Gunderson," Emily snapped at him. "You know that, don't you?"

He shrugged and grinned.

"You wouldn't be the first woman to tell me that," he replied. "But you don't have to live a life of quiet depression while you grow old and eventually die. There are a lot of things out there you could do. Doubly so, since you obviously don't need the money."

"So are you asking me on a date, or to be your partner?" she pressed now, studying his face.

"Neither," he said. "Maybe both. Who knows? I only met Emily Reed last week, so I don't know that much about who this woman has become. Only who she used to be, but that was a long time ago."

Emily leaned back and sipped at her coffee.

"Forty-one only feels old because you remember being twenty," Gunderson continued. "I'm only a couple of years behind you, but we've both already had interesting lives so far. However, I have a whole life still in front of me, doing what I do and trying to make the world a better place."

"Let me think about it," Emily replied ambiguously.

Gunderson nodded and finished his coffee. He slid out of the booth and left the last of Flanagan's dirty money on the table top to cover the bill and a nice tip.

"Take all the time you like, Emily." Gunderson put his hat on and then tipped it it to her. "World's not getting any better, anytime soon, so I won't be out of work."

She watched him with inscrutable eyes, silent. Gunderson smiled back at her and made his way to the door of the diner.

He'd survived Roosevelt, Hitler, and Ike. If he ever heard from Emily Reed again, he figured he could survive her, too.

VEILED

THE GUNDERSON CASE FILES (005)

VEILED

GUNDERSON FIGURED that about half of his cases these days came from his old friend Joyce and a few other friends sending people his way. Folks with serious problems and enough cash to afford the rates he charged for helping solve them. Those cases were usually a safer bet than when strangers walked into his office from out of the blue.

Especially this gentleman.

Looked Greek. Swarthy complexion. Dark hair just long enough to show curls. Trimmed mustache Average size, but he moved like a caged animal as Gunderson's secretary/pitbull Annabelle escorted the fellow into the office and closed the door behind her as she left. Back to her book on early Gothic authors.

Gunderson gestured the man to sit as he stood, moving to refill his own coffee mug and to pantomime to the man asking if he wanted any.

The stranger shook his head.

Gunderson sat back down and contemplated that this pot should have gotten poured down the drain already, but he was too lazy to make a new one, and not enthusiastic enough to head down to the bar or a nearby restaurant for a slice of their coffee.

Probably his third mistake today, right after getting out of bed and coming into the officer.

"My name is Argyros Stefanidis, Mr. Gunderson," the man introduced himself.

Yup. Greek. Maybe translated into English as Stevenson, if Gunderson was doing the philology right.

Gunderson nodded over his coffee and watched the man.

Walk-ins were always a hazard. Joyce had really good instincts for people, which was why he trusted her to filter out the weirdos. She knew most of the bad people in this town from before her first husband—the gangster—got himself killed.

Still, the law required him to keep an office and to keep the door unlocked during business hours. Something about this man just rubbed Gunderson the wrong way. Maybe his cologne. Or that gleam in his eyes.

"I need your help finding a woman, Mr. Gunderson," Stefanidis continued. He caught the gleam in Gunderson's eye and smiled. "Not for that, sir. She is a monster and must be stopped."

"From?" Gunderson asked.

"I beg your pardon?"

"What must she be stopped from doing, Mr. Stefanidis?" Gunderson asked. "It's a free country here, so people are generally allowed to do most things, assuming that there aren't already laws in place to cover certain behaviors. At which point the police should get involved, rather than a private citizen such as myself."

Stefanidis smiled wryly. It already felt like they were dueling on a dance floor with sabers.

"How well do you know your Hellenic history, Mr. Gunderson?" the man asked now, growing serious again.

"I've read Bullfinch and maybe a few other books," Gunderson conceded without admitting much.

Unlike some private detectives, he didn't dabble in chess or music. Books kept the mind sharp, and refilled that creative bucket in the head that a PI needed to be able to make certain intuitive leaps.

"Are you familiar with the story of Medusa?" Stefanidis asked, eyes almost glittering with some inner emotion that Gunderson couldn't identify. The voice got a little husky and breathless, like a weird combination of rage and lust, with a fine veneer of fear dry-brushed along the edges.

"Beautiful woman, raped by Poseidon, transformed by Athena," Gunderson said. "Perseus killed her as part of his heroic quest, back in Bronze Age Greece."

"Correct," Stefanidis acknowledged. "He cut off her head and used it as a weapon, eventually giving it to Athena for place in her shield, the Aegis. According to legend, he was the great-grandfather of Heracles, as well."

"What's that got to do with Los Angeles or the Eisenhower Administration, Mr. Stefanidis?" Gunderson asked coolly, now.

"Medusa was one of three sisters, Mr. Gunderson," he said. "Euryale and Stheno were her elders, all daughters of Phorcys, the sea god and his cousin Ceto, a sea goddess."

"Sure," Gunderson said with a *whatever* kind of voice.

He hadn't been hired by this mook yet, so he wasn't getting paid for a history lesson. On the other hand, his daily rate was already climbing as the conversation proceeded.

"Perseus killed the one, Medusa, but the other two escaped, Mr. Gunderson," Stefanidis continued. "Terrible, minor goddesses with snakes for hair, sharp fangs, and brass hands."

"So?"

"So my organization has been hunting those monsters

and others for more than thirty-three centuries, Mr. Gunderson," Stefanidis concluded with a terrible gleam in his eyes. "Making the world safe for mankind by destroying all those old gods."

It was on the tip of his tongue to ask how you actually killed a god, but Gunderson had read other mythologies as well. Losing the golden apples had nearly killed off the Norse Aesir. Maybe all those creatures everywhere were just powerful sorcerers who took on vestiges of godhead compared to the lesser beings they encountered?

"Killing them?" Gunderson confirmed.

"They must all be destroyed, Mr. Gunderson," Stefanidis assured him, voice getting loud before a hand slammed on the desk. "Otherwise, they will return and attempt to reign over us all again."

Gunderson had almost leaned across the desk to throw his coffee in the man's face before he realized that it was all a performance.

Hopefully a performance and he wasn't dealing with a complete nutcase today. Man seemed to have anger issues and a lot of emotional baggage, none of it good.

Gunderson tried to make it to church more frequently than Easter and Christmas, but he'd never really been a religious kid. Growing up and doing the things he'd done and seen hadn't interested him in deeper devotions.

"Let me get this straight in my own head," Gunderson focused on the man. "Ancient gods and goddess might still be around, however many centuries or millennia after their culture has ended?"

The man nodded sagely.

"And you belong to an organization dedicated to hunting them all down and killing them?" Gunderson continued

Again, the nod.

"And you obviously think that one of them is living in

Los Angeles, today," he said to a third nod. "Why do you need me?"

"She can hide from my kind, Gunderson," Stefanidis said. "We take powerful oaths when we join, and hunt with both modern weapons as well as ancient one that have the power to commit *deicide*. It is not enough to just shoot a god. They can heal from such wounds. Perseus needed a magical *harpe* from Zeus, a powerful sword made of enchanted steel in an era of bronze weapons, to behead Medusa."

"So she'll smell you coming a mile away?" Gunderson translated that out of all the flowery bullshit into something concrete, just to make sure he had the man's number.

Sounded like a load of horse ----, but it had tickled his curiosity. Gunderson wouldn't mind being paid by this yahoo, or all his friends, to track down and meet a verifiable goddess.

"That is correct, Mr. Gunderson," Stefanidis nodded, his face finally calm again after all the emotional histrionics earlier.

"Los Angeles is a big place," Gunderson pointed out. "Single needle, enormous haystack."

"We have a few clues," the man said. "And a device that will work as something of a lodestone. We need you to find her and confirm that it is her, so that we can swoop down and annihilate this creature before she can escape us again."

"Again?"

"We came close in London in 1931, Mr. Gunderson," Stefanidis preened. "But for a stroke of bad luck, we would have destroyed her entirely, but she slipped away at the last, having turned one of my brothers to stone as she did."

"Huh," Gunderson interjected, mostly as a placeholder. Might be worth looking that sort of thing up, at least in his spare time.

He quoted the man a rate for daily and expenses. It was high, on the presumption that if they were on the level, the organization was ancient enough that they ought to have some gold vaults lying around.

And the man came across something of an asshole.

Got the fool out of the office quickly enough, with a large chuck of cash up front and a promise of regular updates, plus a list of target locations, and a nifty, brass compass. Except that it didn't point north.

Right now, it didn't point any direction. Apparently, you had to be pretty close for it to pick her up through whatever magics she was using to disguise herself.

Not for the first time, Gunderson considered permanently locking the outer door to his office and just relying on Joyce and her friends to send him business, but the city and the state had requirements, and even sent inspectors around regularly to make sure men and women like him were following the letter of the law.

But days like today really tempted him to going back to that one job as a short order cook.

GUNDERSON HAD FOLLOWED his nose to the student union at a local college. Specifically, the dining area. The man he wanted rarely ate with the rest of the faculty, saying that he didn't want to risk turning into a stodgy, old fart like the rest of them, even though he was barely thirty.

But Tony Gythiell was special. Brilliant. The kind that had started college early, finished fast, and then gone on and gotten a PhD in literature before he was twenty-two, focusing on the ancient stuff. Man didn't read Egyptian hieroglyphics all that well, or ancient Sumerian, but near as Gunderson could tell, if those ancient Greeks spoke it or read it, he could too. Plus a bunch of more modern languages.

Gunderson had snuck into a class on Homer one day, just to kill time, and watched Tony put a word up on the board. Then translated it into ancient Greek. Modern Greek. Old English. Old Russian. Modern Russian. Italian. Portuguese. French. German. Arabic. And Ideogramic Chinese, just to be a shit.

Tony looked up from his burger and took a deep bite as Gunderson approached. Probably to make Gunderson do all the talking at first. Tony liked to consider his answers.

In person, he was average height, with thinning, brown hair that would turn into a ring by the time he was forty. Thick glasses. Bit of a paunch in spite of playing fiercely competitive badminton regularly.

Gunderson took the open chair across from the man and ignored the two students down a little holding hands and cooing at each other.

"So I have a most interesting case," Gunderson began without preamble as Tony chewed slowly. "Fellow seems convinced that various Greek gods and goddesses survived the rise and fall of Rome, and are still running around today."

From the look on his face, Tony was suddenly regretting a mouthful of juicy burger that prevented him from talking.

Gunderson just smiled at the man. Paybacks could be an utter bitch.

"I've been hired because supposedly one of them is currently residing in Los Angeles somewhere," he continued, beaming at the torture he was inflicting on the younger man.

"Who?" Tony managed without spitting food.

"Stheno," Gunderson said. "Medusa's sister."

"Oldest sister," Tony automatically corrected him as he chewed faster.

Gunderson stole a couple of french fries and nodded.

"Any chance the man's right?" Gunderson asked.

Tony shrugged and finally swallowed.

"If they are gods as the Greeks might have understood them, probably not," he replied. "But who knows what sorts of beings there might have been in those days. Even today, we encounter certain phenomena we cannot explain, save falling back on that age old hand-waving of magic."

"Some of that magic works," Gunderson pointed out.

"True, but there have been so many con men over the ages that separating the wheat from the chaff is nearly impossible without a guide who already knows," Tony said, snatching at his fries before Gunderson got greedy.

"Know any?" Gunderson asked, pulling that spiffy compass out and laying it on the table between them.

Externally, it looked like any other. A brass cylinder, chopped off, with some sort of silver watch face over the top and a needle made of something black and shiny. Gunderson gave it a quick whirl, just to set it spinning. He'd done the same in his office, and eventually friction had caused it to stop, but nothing else.

"That is to help you find her?" Tony asked, a little amazed. But then, he read the stuff, probably only dreaming that those sorts of beings had really existed outside of someone's fertile imagination.

To suspect that they had been real. Were real. Were still around?

"Only once I get close enough," Gunderson replied. "Got other tidbits and places to look, but figured I should get a little more background than the man who hired me had been willing to provide."

"All right," Tony said. "But since you interrupted my lunch, you get to sit and watch me cram it all down my gullet. Then we will go back to my office and I will have some questions."

Gunderson nodded.

Didn't take long, and then they were in a rat's nest of books, filling shelves on every wall and stacked on the floor and any available surface that would hold them. Without all the clutter, it was probably a nice office. Right now, it felt like a broom closet.

But Gunderson had worked with Tony Gythiell before, so he quickly filled in most of the big details, leaving out names and critical things. Tony listened like a jury deciding on a death penalty case, silent and observant, before he rose and started rooting around in one of the piles.

Eventually, he pulled out a stack of papers in a manila envelope.

"Here, you will need to read this," he announced, thrusting the bundle into Gunderson's hands.

"What is it?"

"The second to final draft of a book I am publishing," Tony said. "The final is at the publisher right now, but nothing significant changed from that. I found a stash of ancient Arabic texts that were direct translations of older ones written in Aramaic, which were themselves versions of the original Greek. Understand that the period from Perseus to Socrates is just about nine centuries, give or take a few dates we can only estimate. Homer was writing a few hundred years after the Trojan War, which was roughly one generation after Heracles and his Great Labors. Perseus is his great-grandfather, so I would guess that he slew the Medusa in about 1300 BC. A lot of interpretation can happen in that time, but the Christian scholars were at great pains to make the Greeks look bad, so they messed everything up on purpose. The Arabic scholars had much less of an ax to grind, so their translations are much more true to the source material. There will be things in there that you will need, if you are really going to meet a daughter of Ceto."

"So it might not be hokum?" Gunderson asked.

"What is truth, you old fart?" Tony grinned. "Have you been able to touch a thing and say 'This is truth'?"

"Nope, but a four thousand year old goddess?"

"What other strange shit have you had to deal with, Gunderson?" Tony got serious now. "I've heard a few of your stories. And all I have to do is read the newspaper to know that there are more things in heaven and earth than are dreamed of by our philosophies. But I also want the whole story when you get done. Maybe we'll write it as a modern fable or something, changing the names of the guilty?"

"We're all guilty of something," Gunderson agreed.

But he got out of Tony's office pretty quickly after that. With promises of after-action reports.

Right now, he had a rendezvous with a goddess.

GUNDERSON FOUND himself at a dinner club, of all places. He'd worn one of his better gray suits, fitting in with the bankers around him as the manager saw him to a quiet table tucked into a corner, with a bad view of the bandstand and a pretty good view of the dance floor.

If he felt like dancing.

It had not yet become a compulsion to pull out the compass and spin it to see if he was really alone, but Gunderson did so anyway, holding it in his hand, close to his chest and below the level of the table as he was finally alone.

It twitched, which almost made him jump.

Every time before, the needle had just spun and spun, but now it hiccuped as it circled. Not much, but Gunderson's nerves were a little frazzled after reading Tony's manuscript.

Beautiful sister who was also a very minor goddess. Medusa had been in Athena's temple as something more than an attendant and less than a priestess. That punk Poseidon had seen her and, like all the big gods, decided that might made right. Nobody could stop him, so he showed up and raped the woman, right there in the middle of the temple floor.

Where Gunderson got pissed was when Athena blamed the victim for her rape. Sounded a little too much like some of the men he'd known around here, asking what a woman might have been wearing that provoked a man to rape her.

Given a few moments of thought, Gunderson had just assumed that the story had been written by a man and gave him an excuse to blame a woman for something like that.

He wondered if Zeus or one of the other big players had gotten involved at that point, leaning on Athena to go after Medusa instead of Poseidon. Sweeping it under the rug. That *never* happened in Los Angeles, by the way.

When the two sisters had gotten mad over everything, Athena had turned all of them into monsters. Snakes for hair. Fangs like Stefanidis had said. Brass hands, which made no sense but was probably a cultural reference he'd missed, like velvet gloves and iron fists.

Athena sounded like a royal bitch, after reading some of the things attributed to her. Gunderson wondered if the woman was just jealous and catty about other goddesses, and had possibly even told Poseidon to go and rape Medusa as an excuse to get any competition out of the way.

Change the names and the places, and it wasn't much worse than Henry VIII or even some of the local politicians Gunderson had been forced to work around to see justice done.

But now Gunderson had a problem.

Everything had been theoretical until this very moment. A joke between guys at a bar sort of thing.

Except that his little compass had suddenly found something. Gunderson wondered if Stefanidis would have been better with something more like a divining rod, that kind of got brighter or dimmer as it saw. Or maybe this was an ancient magic and they'd only found one way to make it work?

He suspected that a beautiful woman turned into a monster with snakes for hair had to have developed some sort of magic of her own to hide her from hunters like Stefanidis.

Four thousand year old game of cat and mouse?

She was supposedly a goddess. Eldest sister of doomed Medusa, cursed with the same power to turn men to stone at a glance. Couldn't leave a trail of statues in her wake without someone starting to whisper things about her, so Gunderson figured she'd look like any other woman.

A waiter arrived. Gunderson ordered a carafe of house red to go with a big porterhouse that Stefanidis was buying for him. Bread got delivered and he concentrated on buttering it just right.

About the time he had finished his salad, a slab of medium-rare beef arrived, with mashed potatoes and veggies in more butter. He dug in and settled himself to see what the evening would bring.

The lights went down halfway about that time as the band started some background music. Mostly just everyone getting warmed up and happy. He'd arrived just in time to be able to eat before the show. His steak was vanishing quickly as the brass grooved through some classics, Gershwin and the like.

His plate disappeared about the same time the lights dropped to near darkness. The drummer started a quiet roll on his snare as a spotlight hit the other side of the stage area and she emerged.

Ye gods.

The woman looked to be average height, but projected a self-image that was nine feet tall. Curvy and voluptuous. Thirty-six, twenty-four, thirty-six, poured into an emerald gown off one shoulder, with white opera gloves to her elbows and a slash nearly to her right hip.

The red hair, up in something of a bun with what looked like a pair of chopsticks holding it place, was an affectation, as her eyebrows were black.

She reached the center of the stage and the band began a torch song.

The woman opened her mouth and Gunderson understood how Odysseus might have gone off-course for so long.

He wasn't even sure he heard the words, so much as the raw pain of love lost and living forever alone. Spellbound was supposed to be a figurative thing, but Gunderson had met a few spell-binders in his time and could recognize what she was doing to the room.

He reached into his pocket and pulled out the compass, but he had no doubts in him that he had just walked into a fairy tale.

SHE SANG TWO NUMBERS. At least Gunderson thought so. It was hard to think. Hard to resist a woman who might have known the original sirens and learned to sing from them.

Or taught them.

There was no introduction. No patter between numbers. Just two and bang, she left just as silently as she had arrived.

The audience eventually remembered to clap, but they had all sat in stunned silence until she nearly made it to the door backstage.

The woman did not feel like an encore, but Gunderson wasn't sure what she could have done to top that. What anyone could have done.

He finished his coffee and slipped into the side hallway to the restrooms, but turned and hit the backstage entrance. Nobody was around to stop him.

Gunderson navigated around people ignoring him as they had to contend with following up that performance.

Eventually, he found her door.

Samantha Ceto.

Gunderson chuckled under his breath and knocked. Samantha would probably be as close as you could get to Stheno in American English, unless you went for Stephanie. And Ceto had been her mother, a primordial sea goddess from a folk who lived on the water most of the time.

"Come in," a voice came through the wood, so Gunderson opened and slipped just far enough inside to get the door closed behind him.

Dressing room. Hollywood standard sort of thing, where various costumes were on a rolling rack on his right and she sat kind of to the left, watching him in a mirror with lights all the way around it, in case she somehow needed makeup to look better.

She was just the same as she'd been, but in two minutes she had added a veil like a Spanish widow over her red hair.

"You're not one of them," she said out of the blue, piecing gray eyes locked on him like anti-aircraft guns hunting the night sky.

Gunderson froze perfectly still, like a rabbit that had spied a hawk.

"But I recognized your touch anyway," she continued. "You're a local they hired to find me, yes?"

Gunderson nodded, wondering if he had just walked in on his own death.

Not hearing stories about statues left behind wasn't the same as there not being any.

She did--...*something* and the air almost changed hue. The room got colder as well.

"What's your name?" she asked in a perfect mid-Atlantic accent that radio people would have offered human sacrifices to acquire.

"Gunderson," he replied. "Is it okay if I reach for a card?"

She smiled wryly, like they both knew what she could do to him if she felt threatened in any way. But she nodded.

Gunderson went into the hip pocket on his jacket and pulled out a card, stepping forward as though he might hand it to her, but a sudden breeze **INSIDE THE BUILDING** lifted it right out of his hands and **CARRIED IT TO HER.**

Gunderson stepped right back to the door and leaned against it so nobody else could come in.

"A private detective, huh?" she asked.

"That's right," he replied, licking lips suddenly far too dry for the climate and the day.

"Are you a stalking horse, Gunderson?" she pressed, sounding almost playful as she did.

Except that the mouse isn't playing. Just the cat.

"Maybe," he answered truthfully.

Never lie to a woman without a really good reason and no chance of getting caught. Pop had taught him that, once upon a yesterday.

Gunderson felt threads being plucked in his brain.

"What's your story?" she queried, but there was something behind it.

Something big and dangerous, like the woman he was seeing was just an illusion cast by the real goddess.

A veiled one. He smiled at the play on words. She'd hidden from Stefanidis with a magical veil.

"That's correct," she said, apparently reading his mind right now and drawing out what she needed to know.

"Was that you in London?" he asked.

"It was," this being nodded. "They almost got me then."

"Stefanidis would have just been a kid, then," Gunderson observed.

"The magics that they use slow the aging," Stheno spoke through a human vessel now. "He'll live for perhaps three more centuries if nothing kills him along the way. How did you find me, Gunderson?"

"I solve puzzles," he answered, aware of a second set of eyes and ears inside his head, in case he thought to mislead this woman. "Tony's book suggested some things. Stefanidis had a list of possible places you might hide. I know this city. The first two I tried were dead ends, but I knew that going in and mostly just wanted to stretch this out for a few extra days, because of the amount of money I was charging that punk. Still not sure it was enough."

"Oh?"

"Athena," Gunderson said, as if that was all he needed.

It might be. She was possibly four thousand years old.

Samantha Ceto laughed. It was a bitter thing. Shrill and all rusty razor blades.

But she was inside his mind, so she knew what he knew.

"Tony Gythiell sounds like a most interesting man," she observed. "A proper scholar after centuries of fools and con men."

Gunderson couldn't really argue with that point.

"And you don't see me as a monster, Gunderson," she continued.

It wasn't a question. And he had no secrets from this woman. Not if she chose to look.

"You have a few mysteries left to you, Human," she said in a tone that chilled him to his core. "I am not Hera's match when it comes to power."

That was even more frightening to consider, if the big players were still around.

"A few of them remain," Samantha noted. "Stefanidis and the rest of the Perseids have been that successful, down the centuries. Even Poseidon, that bastard who started it all, is no more."

"Really?" Gunderson was shocked.

How do you kill the God of the Sea?

"Your government called it *Operation Crossroads*," she said with a harder snarl than before. "The first was an airdropped nuclear weapon. The second went off underwater and so badly contaminated the test site that they never could clean it enough for a third. What they didn't realize was that there was a dead god in the middle of it, and that was part of the cause of such an ecological disaster. Thankfully, they never did try a third time."

"How the hell was Poseidon so stupid as to swim into the middle of a bomb zone?" Gunderson asked, shocked.

You could kill a god with an a-bomb?

"He misunderstood the power involved, Gunderson," Samantha replied levelly. "We all did. Until now, there have never been anything that could really hurt us, save the ancient magics we are all masters of, or weapons from that era. This is different. In addition to killing each other, you Humans could kill everyone and everything, even beings most of you have no idea exist."

Gunderson was glad the door was holding his weight now. She could have knocked him over with a feather otherwise.

Or turned his silly ass to stone.

"What happens if they do kill all of you?" Gunderson asked. "Stefanidis and his pals."

She shrugged.

"Possibly Hades claims us for all time," she replied. "I don't know."

He started to say something, but her eyes glowed and a spike of pain nailed him to the door for a long second. It felt like the worst hangover he had ever survived, magnified tenfold.

"So what will you do, Gunderson?" Samantha Ceto, minor sea goddess and oldest sister of three asked in an inhuman voice.

Gunderson didn't have an answer. Out in the audience, he had been thinking how badly this woman had been screwed by Athena, for the simple of issue of her sister not being powerful enough to stop Poseidon's rape. Stheno had chosen to stand with her sister, and be punished by a jealous Athena.

"Others will come if you escape," he said. "When you escape."

"When?"

"I was hired to find you," Gunderson said, aware of her hands in his mind. "Nothing more."

"He will expect you to guide him to me if I do not flee immediately," Samantha said, sounding more like a woman and less like a—…whatever she was.

"A goddess," she filled in the gap in his vocabulary.

"Yeah, but what does that even mean?" Gunderson fired back at the woman. "Sure, immortal. Powerful sorcerer of some sort who can do things to my mind as easily as she did to that audience out there. What does a goddess even do, if the culture that worshiped her is gone?"

That seemed to hit her back, right between the eyes, but

Gunderson didn't suppose she met many people who didn't fall all over themselves to worship her.

Or hunt her.

Samantha Ceto, aka the Goddess Stheno, was just a problem to solve, sought by a man who made a living defeating puzzles.

"She survives, Gunderson," Samantha replied in a quieter voice. "She hides from the day, because people who see the real me recoil in terror and reach for swords or guns."

"When was the last time you turned someone to stone?" he probed now. "Not counting 1931."

"Not counting 1931?" she asked, pausing as she considered the question. "1793, when I had to flee Paris ahead of the Revolutionary Tribunal. Similar circumstances, but that was just a mob, and not one of the Perseids getting close."

"Can it be undone, this stone thing?" he asked, again, mostly because he was a guy who solved puzzles.

"It cannot, Gunderson," she smiled serenely. "It is your death if I do."

"Then I'd rather you didn't," he said honestly. "I still think you and your sisters got the bum end of the deal, however long ago, but there's not a lot I can do about it right now. Rape is a crime of power, not sex. And you had it perpetuated on all three of you as much by Athena as Poseidon. Is she still around?"

"She is, but I have not encountered her in or her minions in centuries," Samantha replied.

"Really?" he asked angrily. "Didn't she send Perseus in the first place? You're trying to tell me that Stefanidis and his ilk aren't her minions, however they might deny it or try to hide it?"

It was fun, watching her slip onto the back foot now, so shocked that he actually saw her illusion start to fade a little.

Enough to make out movement hidden inside the illusion of her hair. Red snakes, just like the stories said.

"What would it gain her?" Samantha demanded.

"To be the last god on earth?" Gunderson laughed cruelly. "Nothing and nobody would be able to resist her if she decided to unveil herself to the modern world. Assuming, that is, that Ike and Khrushchev didn't both gang up and nuke her into hell."

"I see where you think we were punished by her out of jealousy," Samantha said in a quieter voice.

"Poseidon walks into her temple and rapes a minor goddess right where she's got to be able to see it?" Gunderson felt the anger welling up inside him. "You don't think she knew? Or maybe suggested it to him in the first place? You three were supposedly legendary beauties. How many women did she or Artemis turn into monsters, merely for rivaling them?"

"Many," Samantha whispered. "Terrible was her ire."

"So your sister was set up," Gunderson said. "Old bitch wanted Perseus to be able to do what he did, so she needed some monsters. What better way to get them than to line up all her aunts and cousins and make them over?"

He watched the woman fall into stunned silence. Again, her hair moved of its own volition.

"Would you like to see the truth, Gene Gunderson?" she asked now.

"Is it lethal?"

"Only if you anger me."

"And?"

She smiled. The illusion faded and he saw her as Athena intended. The face grew longer, with a sharp chin and teeth more like a cat. A forked tongue flickered out and he wondered what kisses would be like. The skin turned a green similar to her gown.

Dozens of red snakes rested uneasily atop her head, moving and hissing.

Those gray eyes were the same, but the pupils slitted vertically like a snake as well.

But she was still a woman, however hideous Athena had transformed her face. Still had those curves and that chest threatening to spill over her bodice. He supposed that the snakes would be venomous, if he was close enough to kiss her, but they might just taste his hair and skin instead of killing him.

He shrugged. Goddess or not, she was still a woman.

The illusion returned. Torch singer in a nightclub gig. Gunderson took a deep breath and celebrated still being alive.

"So now what?" he asked.

"You could tell him you didn't find me," Samantha offered.

"No, I could not," Gunderson countered.

"No, I don't suppose you could," she agreed. "Not a man like you, Gunderson. Your honesty would prevent it, even now."

Gunderson nodded. A man doesn't have much in this world, save his reputation.

As an old mentor had once said: "You don't own anything that you can't carry with you at a dead run."

His word was his bond, simple as that.

But this woman was still being raped four thousand years later.

"I will tell the man I located you," Gunderson said. "Obviously, you didn't notice, because I wasn't turned to stone."

"He will demand that you lead him to me," Samantha reminded him.

"Yes," Gunderson agreed in a voice as cold as night. "He will."

And discovered that even ancient goddesses could shiver at the tone of his voice.

GUNDERSON MET Stefandis in the parking lot.

He'd gone home and slept on it. Slept like a baby even, which told him that his instincts were either right, or being manipulated by a being so powerful that she could make him do anything she wanted.

Gunderson wasn't sure there was a difference there, except that Tony's work had leaned heavily on those same themes. A woman raped, and then punished for it seemingly forever, while the man walks away scot free.

Some things just didn't sit well with Gunderson.

The building was a nice theater on the east side of downtown, slipped in where an old farm had been taken out, but not so valuable that it needed to be turned into offices or homes yet. Just a place with a large parking lot.

Stefanidis emerged from his car with an old bowler on his head and a natty suit with a European cut, rather than English or American. But that made sense if the man had Greek heritage. For a moment, Gunderson even saw a sword in a scabbard on his hip, but then it vanished.

Two days ago, he would have been impressed by such an illusion.

Maybe.

"She is here?" he demanded in a breathless tone.

"I believe so," Gunderson agreed. "I saw her show last night and the compass registered something. I didn't understand what until she started to sing."

"Magical?" Stefanidis asked.

"You cannot begin to imagine," Gunderson said. "I knew right then it was her. Tonight, I made reservations in your name. By the way, if anyone asks you are a Greek Consul, okay?"

"A diplomat?" Stefanidis asked with a chuckle. "That is a role I have played, but it has been a long time."

Gunderson nodded. Samantha had suggested that Stefanidis might live three hundred more years. If so, and he appeared to be in his late-thirties now, Argyros Stefanidis might have served the Ottomans in such a role a century or more ago.

"This way," Gunderson led them to the door and introduced Stefanidis to the manager, who immediately began fawning over the man.

They were seated at the top of the arc formed by the dance floor, just about exactly at the center of the room that would be facing the siren when she began to sing. There would be nothing between them but open darkness.

After the first round of champagne was delivered, Stefanidis was all smiles.

"Yes," he said, gesturing. "It will be perfect. I will rush her when she starts to sing and she will never see it coming until my sword cleaves her in twain."

The salad was exceptional. The steaks probably hand-picked by the chef when he knew he had a diplomat in the audience. Gunderson filled up and enjoyed himself.

The lights were lowered for the opening numbers and Gunderson refilled his wine glass. He had considered dessert, but nothing on the menu could compare to what was coming, so he'd skipped it and watched Stefanidis enjoy a bowl of chocolate ice cream delivered by the manager himself.

The whole house fell silent as the room went dark. It was

as though the crowd could already smell something in the air.

To Gunderson, it seemed like he could taste the perfume she had been wearing last night. Bright and floral, like the first roses of spring and the last apple blossoms.

Life itself, emerging from a woman who so many considered an avatar of Death.

Samantha Ceto walked out onto the stage and he could feel her eyes find him, in spite of the spotlight in her eyes and the darkness of the room. Maybe the snakes knew his cologne.

She began to sing.

Last night had been an amazing performance by a special woman. It paled as she wove her spell now.

Everything fell still except the musicians behind her. Samantha seemed to glow with her own inner fire.

Across the table, Argyros Stefanidis had turned so that he could slip easily off his chair and draw his sword, but first he had pulled out a device like the compass Gunderson had in a pocket. Gold instead of brass, but otherwise similar. Probably an order of magnitude more powerful, for all it looked like a pocket watch.

Samantha held the note at the end of her first song and Gunderson wondered if the world was ending. A wash of power swept over the crowd that left chills down his spine and goose pimples across this flesh.

She paused and the world paused with her. The musicians all took a deep breath and the second song began.

Gunderson looked over at the would-be Greek Diplomat and noted that the man had frozen, perfectly still even as he should have charged her screaming insults and battle cries right now.

His color had changed. The gray suit was still gray, but it was made of granite now, as was the flesh.

Gunderson slipped from his chair and walked quickly and silently to the front door, hat in hand as though he had forgotten something. At the door, he put his hat on and turned one last time, backlit, just to hear her sing.

Magical.

He made it to the car and had the Mallory in gear as the screams started from the front door, a mob of terrified humanity rushing into the parking lot to escape.

But they had nothing to fear.

Samantha Ceto would vanish tonight, but Stheno had gotten some measure of revenge for all the things Athena had done to her and her family down the centuries.

And if Pallas Athena wanted to come down and talk about it, maybe he'd have to go tell someone at the Department of Defense what you should do if you needed to kill a god.

JUSTICE

THE GUNDERSON CASE FILES (006)

JUSTICE

THIS STORY IS available in the anthology Blaze Ward Presents #5 *"**Crime And...**"* at your regular retailers.

PANDORA

THE GUNDERSON CASE FILES (007)
PANDORA

GUNDERSON SCOWLED MIGHTILY at the woman, but she seemed utterly immune. Perhaps amused. The most dangerous ones usually were.

And she projected an air of *dangerous* underneath a petite innocence that probably fooled most people. Only thing petite about the woman, actually.

He'd checked her head to toe when she walked into the pool hall and made her way over to the bar where he normally set up his secondary office. So had every other man in the joint. All of them had decided that she was completely out of their league—dangerously so—and gone right back to their games or their beers, leaving him alone to face her.

Woman was wearing ballet-slipper flats. Gunderson was seated, but something about her suggested that the lack of heel meant that at six-foot-three he'd still be taller than her if he stood up.

Maybe.

Now, she was seated in the stool on his right, letting her perfume mark off her territory. If he sat here long enough, that would probably include him. Wasn't a scent he knew, but wasn't one he was ever likely to forget. Kinda like lilacs, but sweeter. Got into your nose and started playing tricks on your brain. He'd known a few women like that over the years.

She had a pretty smile. Pretty green eyes in a porcelain face with freckles. Irish from the long, red hair, if he had to guess, but not old Irish, who tended to be dark and small. Viking Irish, from when the Danes came down and invaded everything and then stayed.

She had that look going, too. Invader who had just landed on your beach as was planning to stay a while. Maybe take everything and keep it herself.

"Gunderson," she said simply with a nod.

Wasn't a question. Wasn't prefaced with Mister. So she was smart enough not to include his first name and he didn't know her well enough that she could get away with *Gigi*, like a few women he knew.

But he could see that changing.

Maybe.

Gunderson nodded, remembering the beer he had forgotten in one hand and taking a sip before it got warm and flat. He put it down and studied her.

Long, A-line dress in blue cotton with white spots and dotted lines that took him a second to identify as a constellation map of the southern hemisphere. The dress had darts or something instead of a belt, so it pinched in around her waist and showed off the line of powerful thighs to go with the muscles he could see in her shoulders. Volleyball player who worked with iron, if he had to guess. Competitive swimmers tend to get a V-shape like a man and she was balanced both top and bottom with power.

She also looked like she'd be comfortable in a scale-mail tunic with an axe in one hand and a round shield on her arm, hair braided and back under an iron cap with a long nasal protecting that pretty nose from ever being broken in a fight.

He nodded again. Seemed appropriate, as she was just sitting there letting him get an extra eyeful that everyone else in here was only getting sidelong.

"Professional of personal?" he asked.

Gunderson didn't like the way her eyes lit up. Like maybe *personal* was an option she hadn't expected when she walked in. He cursed himself quietly and made a mental note to stop saying things like that to pretty women in bars.

"Professional," she replied after a half-beat.

She had a body men dreamed of and the voice of a BBC evening newscaster to put you to sleep by. Smooth and soothing, so you had pleasant dreams of sailing off with beautiful dames and sacking Irish monasteries.

He nodded a third time. Technically, this was his other office. More business found him here than back at the one the State of California required him to maintain by law. Most of the time they showed up in cheap suits and shoes past the time they should have been re-soled.

"Beer?" he asked, just because Joe behind the bar was a little antsy right now. Probably never seen a woman this beautiful in here. Or any other places.

"Irish whiskey," she said with a smile, as though playing a part for him and every other guy in here.

Joe flipped a glass and gave her a good pour. She sipped it daintily.

Gunderson took another sip of his ale and watched her. He dropped a sawbuck on the counter for Joe just because it felt like that kind of day.

"You found me," he said announced neutrally, mostly as a way to prod her along on the professional side of things, before she reconsidered *personal.*

Joyce had once explained it to him as competence porn,

but Gunderson didn't figure he had the right plumbing to understand that, so he just nodded at the effect he apparently had on some women and smiled.

More than half of his cases came from Joyce these days. The woman had an amazing number of contacts left over from her old life as a bit-part chorus girl who had married shady money and then inherited it all when associates of her gangster husband killed the man.

She was also one of the few people out there that could get away with twisting a first name like Eugene into *Gigi* without getting punched in the mouth. Last marine who had tried it still walked with a limp.

Personal suggested this woman might like to call him that too. He might even let her get away with it.

"We would like to hire you, Gunderson," she said simply. "Our ship is…off-shore and beyond legal zones, so the authorities won't be of any help. But a crime has been committed and we need your help to solve it."

He'd caught that tiny burr of hesitation when she talked about her ship. He wondered just how far off-shore it really was. Los Angeles was his home these days, but it was also filled with all manner of weirdness that your average suburban housewife—or private detective—never saw. Or wanted to understand. Gunderson didn't care one way or the other, as long as he got paid his daily rate plus expenses.

He couldn't save the world, but he could go a long ways towards cleaning it up, dealing with the various jackasses he ran into along the way.

She didn't look like she needed much help in the physical department, *personal* notwithstanding, so they must need his brains. But solving puzzles was his thing. And occasionally breaking heads.

"How long would I be gone?" he asked ambiguously, not taking the case, but not rejecting it out of hand, either.

Joe wouldn't understand anything, nor would any of the other bums and peons in here as her eyes got cagey. Like he'd already said *yes* and now they were just working out details.

Pretty women can frequently get a guy to do things for her just by smiling at him, but Gunderson wasn't buying it. She'd walked in here in that dress and that smile, *needing* something.

"Perhaps as much as a week," she offered daintily. "We'd of course hire you exclusive during that period."

As in, you probably won't be around LA to do anything for anyone else, but most of his other cases were slow-burn sorts of things, right now. Philandering husbands. Business partners concerned that someone has a secret gambling habit. Those sorts of things that never make the news, but lubricate the wheels of commerce for a private detective.

"Of course," he nodded back, playing her game. "Do you have references?"

It was a rude game to play, but the sudden jolt of surprise in her eyes was telling. Most of his cases came from a friend of a friend. That or Joyce sending them, which was pretty much the same thing.

Asking for references from a total stranger to Los Angeles was something of a low blow, because she wasn't from around here, accent and pretty face notwithstanding. But he resolved crimes for a living.

Not *solved. Resolved.* Sometimes you couldn't catch everyone and turn them over to the cops. Sometimes no crime had been committed. But resolving the puzzle was usually enough for him.

This woman was a puzzle. A Pandora's box of secrets she didn't want to open in front of Joe and everyone else. But she needed Gunderson.

That made it a fine line to walk.

"No," she finally admitted in a quieter voice. At least this was the only honest answer she could give him. That much was certain. "Nobody in Los Angeles could vouch for me."

Just to be a bit of a shit, he leaned into that zone of perfume and let it mark him. But it also got him close enough to whisper to her.

"Can anybody?" he asked with a polite smile that cut through all her obfuscations and denials.

And let her know not to bother trying.

Her gasp of surprise wasn't even audible as far away as her glass of Irish Whiskey, but he was inside that perimeter.

"Nobody that you would recognize," she murmured after a long beat.

They were almost to the pillow talk level of voices now. But nobody else needed to know any more truths about her than that she was a beautiful damsel in distress.

Whether it was actually a devil in a blue dress instead remained to be seen.

"Let's go back to my real office and chat," he said, sliding off the stool.

She took his hand as she joined him.

Yeah, an inch of heel gave him two inches over her flats, but he'd never met a woman who stood six-two and moved like that. She almost felt compact, as long as she was, like she normally stood eight feet tall and had somehow been scrunched down for this.

He let go of her hand before she got any bright ideas and held the front door open for her to precede him out into the spring's afternoon heat.

Gunderson realized that he hadn't even asked her name.

But Pandora would do for now.

GUNDERSON SMILED as he lead the woman into his outer office now.

Annabelle had worked in the aircraft factories a decade ago during the war. She retired, but her husband had died, leaving her with his pensions and life insurance, and not much to do. Gunderson had hired her as a secretary. She said it was just as easy to knit here as at home or the senior center. Or read.

Right now, she just raised an eyebrow at him when he walked in with the tall woman. Then gone right back to her book on marine engine design.

He didn't have to tell her to hold his calls. Nobody ever used this telephone. Every cop and gangster in the city would call Joe the bartender first anyway. And Joe would give them an earfull right now.

So Gunderson showed Pandora into his office and closed the door.

He stopped her from sitting immediately and directed the woman to the other chair, farther from the door. The comfortable one.

He'd recently sawed a half-inch off the back legs on the one most people would sit in. Left you always feeling on the edge of falling over backwards, or forced you to sit forward.

Anything to throw people off and get them out of his office quickly. Too many people meeting him here these days, instead of letting him grill them in front of Joe.

She glanced at the two chairs as she sat and grinned knowingly. He shrugged and moved around to the other side of the desk.

Some private dicks would pull out a pipe or maybe roll a cigarette right now, just to show you how tough they were. Others might pull a bottle out of the bottom drawer and two glasses. He had them, but this wasn't that kind of situation.

He just studied her. She studied him.

"What was the crime?" he asked finally, when it became clear she wasn't going to talk.

"Murder," Pandora replied, eyes and face serious now. "One of the crew is dead and it was not an accident."

"Why me?" Gunderson asked.

"You come highly recommended, even for your kind," she said.

He had a pretty good idea what *his kind* implied, but that didn't let her off the hook.

"And you can't call someone else in because…?" he volleyed that hot potato back into her lap.

"Because we are a tremendous distance from home, Gunderson." Pandora's eyes were hard now. Dark sapphires filled with something terrible and hungry. Probably more like the real woman when she dropped the prettiness to one side. "We can return home in order to deal with it, but then we are not here and things might happen during the long stretch we are not present."

"Where are you really from?" he asked, maybe closer to savage now.

"You wouldn't believe me," she replied.

"I don't have to believe you, miss," he smiled like a rusty razor. "I just need to *confirm* you."

"What do you think the truth is?"

"That you aren't from around here, though I'm not sure what *here* entails," he snapped. "That you got a problem and need *my kind* because I'm close and known to keep secrets. That I solve problems, and then keep my mouth shut about it afterwards because the check cleared. Am I getting warm?"

She leaned back and drew a breath. He watched her eyes and wondered if he might need to flip the desk over on top of her then go for his Smith and Wesson Model 29, tucked comfortably under his left arm.

"Violence is not necessary," she said, both arms coming up defensively. "No shooting."

"Can you read my mind, too?" he rasped at her.

"Only the surface emotions," she said after a moment. "And only in moments of great power. Normally your kind look like a color to me. Gray with hints of gold in your case, but bright scarlet just then."

"My kind?" he growled.

If she was going to hire him, she was going to give him some level of truth. Trust cut both ways, after all.

"Humans," she finally admitted.

Which made her…not-human.

Gunderson wondered if the word had gotten out among the aliens that walked the streets of L.A. as well.

He'd met some in this line of work. Cashed the checks. Kept his mouth shut.

How far had word gotten around?

"So now we're getting somewhere," he said, relaxing back into his chair.

Just for the hell of it he pulled the bottle and both glasses, holding them out towards her in invitation.

Pandora nodded and he poured them each a shy finger. Mostly a social lubricant to bond over, rather than anything else. Like drinking to forget.

Gunderson didn't have much to forget. He'd already done most of that, so that now the war was just a boring blur of things, as long as he didn't poke and pry at any specific event. He'd heard that most men had been able to compartmentalize themselves on the long sail home, burying things that they intended to never talk about again. A few, like him, had mostly failed, while the rest had mostly succeeded.

Kids these days didn't need to know the truth. We saved the world from evil men, and that was enough.

She took her glass and matched his sip.

"I can't keep calling you Pandora in my mind," Gunderson announced. "What's your Earth name?"

She blinked, but he wasn't sure which part got to her.

"Bailey," she said quietly. "Bailey Hajeli. You're taking this well."

"Not my first rodeo, Miss Hajeli," Gunderson toasted her with his glass and drank another sip.

"So we'd been told," she toasted him back with just a hint of a grin on those kissable, red lips.

On the surface, two old friends having a drink. There would need to be a lot more sexual tension in the air for it to look like a date, but Gunderson had no idea how many tentacles she might have in her native form.

And he wasn't Japanese.

"And your ship is…out there?" he asked, gesturing upward with his glass.

"It is," she replied evenly. "But we can get there directly from here."

Oh, we can, can we?

"I should charge you double my normal rates," he mused.

"That's acceptable," she smiled petitely. "You are our best hope for solving this. Otherwise, we will have to return home and who knows what we might miss."

"Khrushchev is crazy, but not entirely stupid," Gunderson noted. "Mao is making everyone in DC nervous right now, but considering what we've done to them for the last hundred or so years, I can't say I blame the man. Ike's pretty good, but his Vice President is a crook. Petty wars everywhere, but hopefully the smart ones stop the crazy ones from unleashing Armageddon."

"Yes, that pretty much sums it up," Bailey replied, but in Gunderson's mind Pandora might still be more appropriate.

"You folks planning to invade us at some point?" Gunderson asked.

Mostly, that was curiosity. They wouldn't likely make as big a mess of it as humans did on their own.

"No, but we also aren't going to invite you into space with us, either," she replied firmly.

The woman was relaxing now. That was good.

"Fair," Gunderson replied. "I wouldn't. You'll get me back when I solve things? Or can't?"

"Right here in this office, if that's acceptable?" she asked. "Or someplace better."

The twinkle in her eyes was back. The look that suggested she might drop him off at his apartment building and then come up for a nightcap.

Personal.

He finished his glass and left it one the desk as he rose.

She reached into a hip pocket that hadn't been obvious before and pulled out an envelope, counting bills and then just handing it to him.

"Expenses and such," she said with a grin.

Too many bills, but he suspected he was about to earn them.

Gunderson just studied her for a long moment, memorizing this woman, and then walked to the door.

"Annabelle," he said as he opened it. She looked back. "I'm going to be out of town for a week or so, if anyone comes looking. Can you swing by my place and water the plants?"

He didn't have any plants, but she'd deal with his mail, his landlord, and maybe his bank if there were problems. She already handled most of his communications with folks. He handed her the envelope, not figuring he'd actually need money where he was going.

She glanced past him inquiringly, and then smiled.

"Will do," she said with a nod.

Gunderson closed the door and moved to the shades, flipping them closed as well. He had a fourth-story office, but there were towers all around and he had no idea what might be visible from the outside.

He turned to the woman and found her standing already.

"I'm going to change now first," she said, studying him intently. "Then we will traverse to the ship."

Gunderson nodded and licked lips gone suddenly dry. He'd already memorized the beautiful woman's shell, just so he had that. Whatever she turned into now would be the real person.

Whatever that was.

She looked up at the ceiling once to measure it. It was an older building with ten foot ceilings and pressed tin he usually ignored, except when a spider dropped onto his desk.

Bailey was wearing a thing on her left wrist that was too big to be a bracelet, but not long enough to be a Viking bracer. Silver, with an uncut red stone in it, maybe three inches long and made of bands of metal that looked hammer-welded together. She pressed her right middle finger to the stone and held it there for a moment. Around them saw the room simply lit up like sunrise.

When his eyes cleared, Gunderson was surprised that she hadn't changed much. Still had long red hair. The freckles were maybe a little more faded, but the eyes were brighter.

Her smile was a bit tentative though, as one might expect considering that she was now about nine feet tall. At least the dress had resized with her, so he wasn't dealing with a beautiful, naked woman as well, whatever species she really was.

Looked human, and that was enough for now.

Kind of distracting, with the points of her breasts almost on level with his eyes, but she was wearing something under the dress to contain them. Assuming they acted like human ones.

Bailey held out her left hand to him and Gunderson stepped close to take it, eyes noting the way that red stone was glowing internally now.

"Ready?" she asked.

He grunted something vaguely affirmative and held his breath.

Pandora pressed the stone with two fingers and a light filled the room again, like her namesake opening her box to the world.

GUNDERSON LOOKED around the room when he finally stopped seeing stars. Metal walls, like he was back aboard a US Navy warship sailing to Africa.

Or he was on the set of one of those pulp science fiction movies. Probably midway on that spectrum. Bailey was still holding his hand, but he stepped away from her now and inspected the woman from enough distance to take in all nine feet of her at once.

Yeah, this was what she normally looked like. The Pandora in the bar had indeed been this same woman squished down to his scale, so she could walk around and not cause more of a ruckus than a beautiful woman in a slinky blue dress on a nice day normally would.

A door slid sideways into a wall and more figures entered. Three of them. All women. All nine feet tall or so, but these were dressed more like a Hollywood costumer would do it, if you told him Greco-Roman warrior women in space.

Tunics in white maybe a little past mid-thigh, with a single band of color around the edge. Red, gold, green.

Leather belts with gold fittings and buckle, sporting a logo he couldn't recognize.

He'd have said Amazons, following the old Scythian model, but those ancients had supposedly burned off one breast when they were young, so as to not interfere with drawing a bow. These women wore what looked like ray guns on their hips, so they could presumably still have their original factory equipment.

He was surrounded by two redheads, a strawberry blond, and a true blond. Some men might have thought they'd died and gone to heaven.

Gunderson figured he had the heavens part accurate. Hopefully he wasn't dead.

"You were successful," the strawberry blond with the red stripe announced in a voice that knew it would sound rude if there was any more disbelief in it. She managed to just tread the line.

The other two women were kind of back and flanking, letting Bailey and Red Stripe talk. He felt like he was standing in a bowl of mountains, looking up. All of them were pretty. Could even pass for human from a great enough distance. Or if a setmaker got tricky and built things to their scale for filming.

Any of them could find work in Hollywood.

"I was," Bailey replied in an equally aloof voice.

Like you could have kept him from wanting to solve a crime surrounded by pretty women? Far better than the pudgy Irish police detectives he usually had to deal with when there was a murder. Red Stripe still looked like a cop, though.

Red Stripe looked him up one side and down the other. Gunderson kind of regretted wearing one of his more rumbled suits, but shit happened and this wasn't the case he was expecting to walk in the door when he got up this morning.

"Hillary Ellet," Red Stripe said, apparently introducing herself as she held out a kodiak-sized mitt for him to shake. "Securitist."

Whatever the hell that was.

He took her hand and sure enough, she went for the power play, squeezing hard on his bones. Had a hell of a grip, too. Gunderson smiled at her.

Then returned the favor.

She had apparently never learned to control submachineguns on full auto at close range while clearing a building. The ray gun on her hip probably didn't generate any recoil.

Ellet's eyes got a little wide, but he stopped before he figured he'd done any permanent damage.

He never stopped smiling. Bailey was just enough behind the woman that Securitist Ellet missed her grin.

Pandora stepped up now, like a referee breaking a clinch and reminding two heavyweights to behave themselves.

"Bronwyn Theryth, Technologist," Bailey said, indicating the redhead with the gold stripe who stayed at a distance and nodded at him. Then she turned to the blond with the green stripe. "Ellis Adwild, Urbanologist."

Gunderson had no idea what the terms meant, but he'd read a book or two. Securitist suggested goon and bodyguard. Maybe boss goon. Technologist sounded like the short, pudgy guy aft tending engines. Urbanologist left no impression, unless she studied cities. Human cities. Human culture.

Adwild looked older than the others, but not much. If Bailey Hajeli could pass for mid-thirties, then Adwild was pushing forty and the other two were probably just straddling thirty.

"What do you know?" Securitist Ellet asked in a professionally-hard voice.

"Murder," he replied. "And that nobody here had the skills or experience to solve it without returning to your homeworld, by which time the trail is cold, the evidence is maybe destroyed, and the crime goes unsolved."

He wondered how well this woman could read the surface of his mind. She recoiled a little, but probably wasn't used to humans this close.

And him not even on a leash.

Gunderson's smile wasn't as friendly now. Didn't figure his aura was, either.

The two quiet ones didn't seem to like Ellet all that much, from the way the three seemed to enjoy his performance. But he was here to do a thing, and by God he would.

He let his scowl speak instead.

"The environment here is clean," Bailey said in a way that didn't suggest he was dirty, so much as scruffy. "I'll show you to your cabin and you can get cleaned up. Then we will reconvene in my office in an hour."

Referee. Heavyweights. Break clean and tow a line. Gunderson nodded.

"Ellis?" Bailey asked.

"Follow me, please," the Urbanologist commanded politely, so he did.

Gunderson found himself in a corridor too wide and pleasant to be a warship. Felt more like a cruise liner running down to Ensenada or something, all bright and spacious. And not just for him. The woman he was walking beside had space overhead.

A few crewwomen noted his passage but didn't speak. All of them were around nine feet tall, even wearing those sandals that laced around your ankle, Greek-style. White tunic. More stripes. Nothing darker than mousy-brown for hair, but all gorgeous.

Died and gone to somebody's idea of heaven.

Urbanologist Ellis Adwild stopped at a little alcove and pressed a button about at eyeball level for Gunderson. The wall retracted to the side and he found himself looking into a room like he would have done it. Not his bedroom, but not that far off. Like they'd taken pictures, then improved everything.

He made a note to reconsider his interior decorating when he got home.

She entered and he followed her. Felt professional, rather than personal. He was fine with that.

"Your closet is here," she pointed. "We tried to make you some clothing in your size and appropriate styles. The restroom is through there and a quick shower will both protect you from our germs, as well as give you chemical treatments that will protect us."

He nodded and watched her depart. Sounded so much better than *sheep-dipped*, but he didn't figure the outcome was going to be much different.

Closet with half a dozen suits. Nicer shoes than he could usually afford. Undershirt and boxers. Socks. Rack of really nice ties. Impressive work, since he hadn't seen a single male here, and they didn't any of them dress like a human from Earth.

Gunderson idly wondered where he was. The moon supposedly had a much lower gravity than Earth, but every scientist in the world was pointing telescopes at it right now, looking forward to the day rockets could get people there. Maybe they were just sitting in space nearby, watching and painted black?

Didn't really matter. He stripped and tossed everything onto the bed for lack of a laundry hamper.

The bathroom was all sorts of fancy, with tile in a complicated pattern that spanned the rainbow, run in an hombre of white at the bottom left to a navy blue so dark it appeared black at the top right.

Thank God the shower had two knobs. He tested them and got the temperature right. Head was even to human scale, so he grabbed the bar of soap and got himself clean by alien babe standards.

Dry, he stepped to the closet, noting as he went by that his old clothes had vanished. He wondered if Pandora had put them back on Earth, or if he was just out that suit. Not a great loss, he supposed, as he'd maybe end up trading them for one of these.

Gunderson was six-three. Broad in the shoulders and tapered. Most suits that fit his upper chest were baggy around the middle, because he couldn't afford custom tailoring and there were only so many inches you could cut out without ruining something.

The first one he grabbed after he got underthings on had been cut to fit him like someone had used a mold. Italian style rather than English, so sleek. Narrow lapels. Four buttons instead of his usual two. Two vents on the sides instead of one in the back.

He'd originally thought it was black, but when he got it into the light it was a polished bronze with gold threads running through it. Didn't feel like wool. Or cotton. Or even silk. Lighter than silk. Warmer than wool, even though the women kept the ship warmer than he would have.

White Archer shirt with button down collar. He flipped though the ties and found one in red silk that looked like something Salvador Dali might have owned. Again, narrow, when a lot of men wore things wider than his hand still.

Gunderson stepped to a full length mirror and wondered

if it was wise letting women who were rethinking *personal* dress him. Might be dangerous.

Even the shoes fit better than any pair he'd ever worn.

That suggested a great deal more forethought than just bipping down to the bar to hire a guy about a thing. Unless they had machines that worked that fast. He was on an alien ship God-knows how far from home. With alien women.

Anything might be possible.

He approached the door and it opened, revealing yet another two-breasted Scythian in white standing across the hallway. Or did you call them corridors on a spaceship?

She was a redhead, with a crimson stripe like Hillary Ellet had, so Gunderson presumed another Security goon, however easy she was on the eyes.

And they did read minds, at least to a degree, because the woman blushed pretty at him and kept her eyes on the horizon.

"You my escort?" he asked.

"Yes, ma'am," she said automatically.

"Lead on."

She turned to her left and he fell into step beside her. The ship was huge, just from the number of steps they took before getting into an elevator.

"Deck five," his guardian announced, rather than pushing any buttons or talking to an elderly black man on a stool.

The room ascended, so he'd been deeper than five. Bigger than a battleship, it seemed.

The door opened and they kept going in silence, save for the slap of this woman's leather sandals on the metal deck.

She opened a door and stayed outside while he went in.

Bailey didn't have a desk like his. She stood behind a waist-high table, except it didn't have any legs, just floating in space. Hillary Ellet, Securitist was standing off to one side, not quite slouching against a sidewall but not all that far removed from it, either.

The walls in here were metal, but had been painted over with a something that involved a lot of swirls and French curves in various colors against a white background. Busy, but not necessarily bad.

Just not his thing.

Both women eyed him with an almost-predatory hunger as he came to rest. Being two-thirds their size didn't help.

"How long ago was the crime?" he asked without any small talk. Mostly just to derail the smiles he saw.

"Forty-one hours," Bailey replied immediately.

Okay, so they weren't slouches, once they realized they had a problem and had to solve it.

"Victim?" he pressed.

Let's get all the details out now, shall we?

"Lory Resby," Bailey said. "Junior Assistant Urbanologist."

Sounded like the sorts of titles you got in government, where every position was fixed by law for pay and seniority. Pecking orders in organizational charts, as it were.

"Crime scene?" he continued down the checklist in his head.

"Her cabin," Ellet spoke up now. "It has remained sealed off since we removed the body."

"So I'll need to see both," Gunderson announced. "How did she die?"

"Physical violence," Ellet said. "Resulting in termination."

Gunderson nodded. Sounded so much nicer than *beaten to death*.

"Suspects?" He asked anyway, not expecting anything. If they knew how to solve crime, they wouldn't have needed him.

"What?" Bailey asked, eyes almost crossed and brow furrowed in confusion.

But Pandora had always been innocence personified. And curiosity, but he didn't need to mention that too loudly, even in his own head.

"Are there people on your crew who didn't like her?" Gunderson asked. "Arguments? Fights? Jealous lovers?"

"There are no men here," Securitist Ellet growled down at him.

Gunderson felt like a yappy Boston Terrier looking up, but those dogs weren't afraid of anything, either.

"So?" he asked in a mild voice. "You think only men are too immature or fragile for that sort of thing?"

His scowl and snarl were entirely mental, as his smile never wavered.

Ellet did growl. Started to move.

"Hillary!" Bailey snapped sharply, like a boss cracking a whip, or an owner pulling hard on a leash in a park.

The big woman subsided, so Gunderson did, too. He'd left his revolver and holster back in the cabin, but didn't figure he'd been too far out of his league if one of these women decided to get physical. He'd been an MP for a number of years, and a Seattle cop before that.

They had still ended up nose to nose, which was probably better than his nose to her decolletage, pleasant as that might be. She had a pleasant smell. More like spring roses than the heady scent of Pandora. Sweet, like tart apples, which was nothing at all like the woman herself.

But we all have secrets, don't we?

Gunderson stepped back, too. Nodded something of an apology to the woman, since she could probably taste it on his mind. He didn't need enemies here. He was just here to do a job and then go home.

Cash the check, keep his mouth shut.

Both women smiled at him now, like they understood.

Crime. Solve. Home.

Professional, not *personal*.

"Body first," he said, mostly to fill the empty air in this strange room.

He expected Ellet to take him, but both women came, so he ended up following the goon and letting Bailey trail him.

The room was like a morgue, and he'd spent too much time in those the last few years, usually because he had the stomach for it so the police let him identify a husband for the wife.

Neither of the women with him looked like they needed a man to open a jar of pickles for them.

There they met the first honest brunette Gunderson had seen on this ship, however barely she rated. Dirty, dark blond on most days, probably. Blue stripe to her tunic. Weird design on her breast he took to be a medical insignia.

"This is Jessica Enneth," Pandora introduced the woman. "Aesculapian."

Close enough to doctor or surgeon, if you translated your Greek and Roman right. And in charge of the corpse.

"Lemme see her," Gunderson growled.

The Doc looked at Bailey, but the boss nodded, so the drawer got slid open. What did it say about whatever their mission was that there were four drawers, all big enough for corpses?

Dead girl. Not his first. At least this one hadn't drowned. Those were always the worst, after they'd been down long enough to start floating when they bloated.

Someone had cleaned her up, but that just spoke to inexperience with crime scenes. All the blood was gone and they'd even gone so far as to rearrange the broken bones close enough to normal. You'd need a skilled undertaker, if you wanted an open casket, but Gunderson didn't figure that was in the future. More likely buried at sea.

He made a note to ask Pandora how they dealt with dead people while on a mission. Didn't matter now, and wasn't anything he could talk about with anyone later, but curiosity is a hard taskmaster.

Young. Pretty enough, too. Redhead, but kept in a modern-looking bob that wouldn't be out of place on any street in LA.

But then, if they could resize themselves to look like *his kind*, Gunderson supposed that an Urbanologist might walk those streets, learning things. As long as she had a raygun handy, or a couple of friends who could all turn into Storm Giants in a pinch…

He smelled her. The whiff was fainter, so he ended up bent over almost close enough to kiss the corpse, terrible images of princes and poisoned apples weighing on his mind. Fall peaches, just on that razors edge of ripe before they fell quickly into rot. Almost not there, but he got it. Imprinted it, just so he had something of the dead woman to take home with him.

Gunderson stood up and studied the three women staring back at him in horrified shock. Wasn't sure what they were seeing. Didn't much care.

"Let's go find her killer," he growled at them.

LORY'S CABIN WAS A MESS. He wanted to say catfight, but then remembered that there were no men on this ship but him, so he went ahead and qualified the struggles that way, keeping all three of the women out in the hallway with the door apparently programmed to stay open. The Doc had followed from the morgue.

He walked back and forth in a half-circle studying things. The bunk was attached to the wall at the top and on one side.

Blood on the floor. Deck. Red blood like his, maybe a little more green before it had started turning black. The smell was close enough for his purposes. Death.

Bed was whatever the equivalent of a full-size was for people nine feet tall, but he was going on ratios here. Damned thing was on a pedestal a little above his waist.

Sheets had been cast every which way.

Struggle.

Lory Resby had not been quietly asleep. And none of her blood was on the bed itself, just pooled across the floor.

"Face up or face down?" he asked, turning to spear Securitist Ellet with a hard look.

"Face down," she said after a moment, still a little white around the gills.

He hadn't asked what a Securitist did if they weren't bouncers. But maybe that was it. Women trained to protect Urbanologists in the field?

Never seen a corpse? Or just not one killed as impolitely as not using a beam?

He turned back and studied the blood. Lots of footprints in it, but the folks responding to the crime wouldn't try to keep it pristine. Didn't know any better.

Bed was big enough for two, if you were snuggled up like spoons. The way the sheets were twisted and knotted suggested that she hadn't been sleeping alone.

"Any cameras or anything that watch rooms?" Gunderson asked over his shoulder.

"There are none," Commander Bailey Hajeli replied, sounding more like a boss now and less like a pretty woman in a bar. "Nor anything other than a button to open the door, but you can lock it from the inside."

He grunted and nodded. Whoever was in here with her had been invited. That much was pretty obvious.

Her closet was in the same place as his, so he walked over and found her laundry hamper. Knelt down and confirmed that peach smell. Stronger here. More robust. Faded quickly on death, apparently.

Peaches. Apples. Roses. That gave him an idea.

Gunderson walked over to the bed, approaching along the wall where the headboard would have been. Because this was a navy ship at sea, there was no nightstand here, so he could avoid getting blood on his new shoes and lean way out with a hand on the frame. Again, he practically buried his nose in the pillow and drew a deep breath. Violets, or close enough for a florist.

He stepped back to the corner, just to frame the whole image in his memory. Played out the choreography in his head like this was a pirate movie or a Zorro remake.

Gunderson nodded and turned to the three faces in the door.

"Let's go to your office, Captain," he announced. "Pretty sure I can solve it."

PANDORA'S OFFICE was still weird. Floating desk with no legs. No chairs. He'd missed the floating wet bar tucked into the corner earlier, or maybe it hadn't been there and she'd ordered it brought in while they were out.

He noted the Irish Whiskey in bottles that probably looked dainty in her hand. Twenty and thirty-year-old bottles, at that, but he supposed that she could probably counterfeit all the hundreds she needed and make them look better than the US government could.

He smiled at the three women and focused on the Doc.

The Aesculapian. Walked right up to her and let her aroma fell his nose as she flinched, just in case.

But she was safe.

Gunderson was beginning to assume that the aliens didn't have as good a sense of smell as humans. Certainly, *his kind* kept dogs around for a reason. He nodded and turned to Hillary Ellet. Securitist.

"So I'm not going to assume you've checked alibis for everyone," he said, just to watch her eyes cross a little. "But that's next."

He turned to the Captain now and just drank in her beauty.

"How many crew do you have, total?" he asked.

"Four hundred and twenty-three," she replied automatically. "Twenty-two now."

"And you are running all the time, right?" he pressed.

"That's right."

"So normally, I would eliminate everyone on duty first," Gunderson said, turning to include all three women. "But I can do you one better. I need the list of all the women who were on the same shift as Junior Assistant Urbanologist Lory Resby. I'm guessing that she was kind of at the bottom of the totem pole, so that would be third shift, US time, right?"

"Well, yes," Adwild replied, still confused.

"And that's the smallest group of women?" Gunderson continued, turning to Bailey now.

"Correct," she nodded, understanding but not following. "Roughly seventy-five, I think."

"I need you to wake them all up, right now, and assemble them for a surprise inspection, Captain," he smiled. "Put them in lines, about ten feet apart like chess pieces."

Bailey nodded to Ellet and that woman departed immediately. The Doc went with her, leaving Gunderson alone with Pandora and all her mysteries.

He walked over to the wet bar and noted that it was low enough for him, so he flipped a highball glass made out of something other than glass from the weight and poured himself a little heaven. He gestured to her and she nodded, so he added a second glass and carried it to where she stood, the desk separating them.

Intentionally separating them.

"You seem awfully certain," she began hesitantly.

"How's your olfactory sense, compared to a human's?" he fired back, taking a sip and letting the liquid wonderful coat his innards.

She sat for a moment and then started typing on the surface of her desk, even though he couldn't see a typewriter. A strange, rectangular glow hung in the air between them, just below her jaw so she was looking down at it and almost staring at him, except she wasn't seeing him.

"Roughly thirty-five to forty percent as sensitive," she offered.

Gunderson wasn't surprised. Average human's nose was two and a half to three times as good, then. Not quite comparable to a dog relative, but headed that way. His sense of smell was even better.

"What did you smell?" she asked, a little in awe of him now. But he'd been on her ship for all of about three hours, and had only known her for about four. Not even that prissy English fellow from literature was supposed to be that good.

But Gunderson would settle for lucky. Always.

"The killer," he replied.

"You can identify us by scent alone?" she asked, a little shocked now.

Gunderson nodded.

"What do I smell like?" Bailey pressed.

He noted a bit of a blush when he looked closer.

"There isn't an Earth-equivalent, per se, but something

like lilacs," Gunderson replied. "Never really smelled anything like it in my life but it's not something I would ever forget."

"Is that so?" she asked, but her voice was meandering over into *personal* now, rather than professional. "And the others?"

"Every woman I've met today has a unique and specific scent," Gunderson said, sipping at the whiskey to keep from adding more details.

Like how the rest were a distant second and third to her smell. Didn't need to say that out loud, even if she might read his mind for it.

Go home, cash the check, keep his mouth shut. That was how the business worked.

She seemed to understand, sipping her own whiskey.

They waited in companionable silence for a time he didn't measure, other than his glass was empty when a quiet tone intruded, like an intercom coming on.

"We're ready for you," Ellet said. "Bay Four."

"We'll be right down," Bailey replied, emptying her glass and leaving it.

He fell into stride next to her and traversed the decks of wherever the hell he was. Down to level eight. More hallways.

Gunderson found himself in an auditorium filled with beautiful Amazons. All white-skinned Danes, from the look, as if that was the only color aliens came in. Did they have different crews for East Asia? For India? For South America or Africa?

Go home, cash the check, keep your mouth shut.

All the women were at attention, eyes on a horizon well above his head, shoulders back, breasts out, feet together.

Gunderson was methodical, so he started on his immediate left and moved like a Mexican gardener mowing the grass. Up and back, each row, each blade given careful attention.

Helped that he'd gotten them all out of bed. Smells were stronger, accentuated by adrenaline and surprise. A smorgasbord of mélange.

He found her about a third of the way in, but kept walking. Kept sniffing. They say fingerprints are unique. Smells should be, as well. At least if they couldn't smell as well as a bloodhound from Earth.

Gunderson completed his rounds and nodded, coming to rest in front of both Bailey Hajeli and Hillary Ellet. So what if he was staring at their breasts as he came to rest, and then looked up.

The ugliest woman in here could be a fashion model or and actress back home, nine feet tall or not.

"You were unsuccessful?" Ellet asked, almost with a hopeful smile on her face.

Pandora's face looked like she had just opened a box. Gunderson let the moment hang for a long moment, perhaps enjoying himself a little too much before he spoke.

"Oh, no," he replied. "I got her. Just wanted to dot all my I's and cross all my T's, since we're talking about a serious crime here."

The two faces reversed at his words, with Ellet turning sour and Bailey smiling now.

"Follow me," Gunderson crooked a finger at them.

He almost felt like Napoleon being trailed by tall men in bearskin hats as he made his way down the row to his target.

Strawberry blond. Gold stripe he took to mean engineering. Young, but not as young as the dead woman. Gunderson wasn't sure if they wore any rank insignia on those tight tunics, but he was judging the woman on her neck and eyes. Thirty and change, but not forty. A Senior

Chief Petty Officer, maybe. The eyes contained that sort of hardness to them.

Gunderson smiled when the woman realized that he had stopped in front of her. He stepped close and confirmed her smell.

Violets. Lovely and dark, reminding him of summer nights. Except that now he'd think about aliens and death, so hopefully she hadn't ruined it for him.

"Her?" Ellet asked, voice climbing in shock.

"Her," Gunderson replied.

Because he was watching, he wasn't surprised at the fist that came up to bash him. Hard woman. The kind that had apparently beaten her lover to death over something. Probably would come out in the interrogation, but hopefully they could handle that himself.

Gunderson couldn't say he'd never hit a woman, but he'd never throw the first punch. The Senior Chief kept that streak alive.

He ducked and slid under the blow, a veteran of too many tavern brawls where nobody liked the Military Police. Didn't have his nightstick with him today, but Gunderson wasn't sure how hard an alien head was.

Didn't matter. He stepped into the woman and threw a full, lunging right into the space where a human would have a belly button.

The aliens apparently had the same soft spot, because all the air went out of her at one and she folded around his fist.

Gunderson was back in Casablanca in his head, so he rotated and drove his left into the back of her ear as it got down where he had leverage. Sounded like a line shot up the middle to clear the bases.

Silence, broken only by the killer collapsing the rest of the way onto the deck and laying still.

He took a fast breath and straightened his borrowed tie.

This was a really nice suit. The one he'd worn this morning probably would have ripped a seam doing that.

Gunderson made a note to inquire with a couple of Italian tailors he knew, and get their opinion on dressing a big Swede.

He stepped back now and turned to the two women.

"All yours," he said loud enough for the rest of the women in here to hear him.

You people might be Storm Giants, but *my kind* are tough sons of bitches, too.

He let that just hang out there, in case the Senior Chief had any friends who wanted to get frisky today.

Looking around, nobody in here was feeling suicidal.

GUNDERSON STUDIED the woman across the table. She'd paid for a week of exclusive time to solve a crime, and refused a refund, so he'd spent a couple of days squiring her around Los Angeles. Parks. Museums. The Boardwalk. The beach. Every night dropping her at a hotel and returning to his apartment alone.

Tonight was steaks. Potatoes. Asparagus in butter. Freshly-baked sourdough. He just enjoyed watching perfect teeth tear the bread after she buttered it. Irish barmbrack drizzled with a whiskey-cream for dessert. The works.

"I don't get you, Gunderson," she finally said when they were alone, walking down the sidewalk towards where that battered '49 Mallory coupe waited.

He ignored the opening and kept walking.

"You don't have a woman in your life," she continued when it was clear he wasn't taking the conversational bait. "You ogle me and all the women on my ship, but never once went so far as to make a pass at any of us."

He gestured at all of her. Tonight, she was back in her ballet flats and starmap dress. It wasn't cold enough that he'd offered to hang his faux-Italian jacket on her shoulders. Plus, he had the Smith under his arm tonight. Wouldn't look good and he didn't feel like arguing with a flatfoot about it.

"You're one of the most beautiful women I've ever met, Bailey," he replied. "But you aren't human. The back of my mind never loses track of that part, even as I watch every other guy goggle and every woman bristle. Your people are out there somewhere, watching Earth and wondering when we're going to blow ourselves up. Or if you need to invade us like some pulp Saturday morning serial and set things to right."

"And?" she demanded quietly.

"And I'm just a guy who solves puzzles, finds things for people, and is good at keeping my mouth shut."

He left it there. Not a lot more to it, when you washed off all the pretty floof around it and got down to the bare bones of the thing.

"I see," Bailey replied.

Before he could react, she spun him towards her, wrapped those powerful arms around his chest, and kissed him. After a moment, he relented and participated.

Alien, sure, but still gorgeous. Still *available*. Pressed hard against his chest now and obviously *willing*.

She broke the kiss and leaned back, smiling at him.

"Is that clear enough?" she asked.

Gunderson grunted something affirmative enough.

"Good," she nodded. "Then right now you're going to take me home and made love to me like the world is ending. After you fall asleep I'll traverse back to my ship and that will be the end of it."

He noted the wicked gleam in her eyes as she spoke.

"It will, will it?" he asked.

"Probably," she grinned after a second.

Gunderson took her hand and started walking. The car was close. The apartment not much further.

And in the end, even Pandora had put a little Hope back into the world.

ABOUT THE AUTHOR

Blaze Ward writes science fiction in the Alexandria Station universe (Jessica Keller, The Science Officer, The Story Road, etc.) as well as several other science fiction universes, such as Star Dragon, the Dominion, and more. He also writes odd bits of high fantasy with swords and orcs. In addition, he is the Editor and Publisher of *Boundary Shock Quarterly Magazine*. You can find out more at his website www.blazeward.com, as well as Facebook, Goodreads, and other places.

Blaze's works are available as ebooks, paper, and audio, and can be found at a variety of online vendors. His newsletter comes out regularly, and you can also follow his blog on his website. He really enjoys interacting with fans, and looks forward to any and all questions—even ones about his books!

Never miss a release!

If you'd like to be notified of new releases, sign up for my newsletter.

http://www.blazeward.com/newsletter/

Buy More!

Did you know that you can buy directly from my website?

https://www.blazeward.com/shop/

Connect with Blaze!

Web: www.blazeward.com
Boundary Shock Quarterly (BSQ):
https://www.boundaryshockquarterly.com/

ABOUT KNOTTED ROAD PRESS

Knotted Road Press fiction specializes in dynamic writing set in mysterious, exotic locations.

Knotted Road Press non-fiction publishes autobiographies, business books, cookbooks, and how-to books with unique voices.

Knotted Road Press creates DRM-free ebooks as well as high-quality print books for readers around the world.

With authors in a variety of genres including literary, poetry, mystery, fantasy, and science fiction, Knotted Road Press has something for everyone.

Knotted Road Press
www.KnottedRoadPress.com

www.ingramcontent.com/pod-product-compliance
Lightning Source LLC
Chambersburg PA
CBHW070529100726
47907CB00004B/1043